BEST FRIENDS
DON'T COME
IN THREES

BEST FRIENDS DON'T COME IN THREES

Joel L. Schwartz

Illustrated by Bruce Degen

A YEARLING BOOK

Published by
Dell Publishing Co., Inc.
1 Dag Hammarskjold Plaza
New York, New York 10017

Yearling ® TM 913705, Dell Publishing Co., Inc.

ISBN: 0-440-40603-X

Printed in the United States of America

September 1985

10 9 8 7 6 5 4 3

CW

To Berky,
my friend and teacher.

1

"Hey, Mom! Where are my sneakers?" I asked as I looked under the bed one more time.

"Where did you put them?" she yelled back from her room.

"I put them right beside my bed."

"Then they should be there."

They should be, I mumbled to myself, *but they're not.*

"They're not here!" I yelled again. "Somebody must have come into my room and taken them. Who's been in my room?" I walked over to the doorway to make sure everyone could hear. "From now on my room will be locked unless I'm in here."

"Richie . . ." said my mother softly as she stood across the hall from me.

I looked up but continued. "When you've had enough, you've had enough!"

"Richie Harmon," my mother interrupted again, "*here are your sneakers.*"

"There is absolutely no reason for anyone to take *my*

sneakers ... my sneakers ... Where did you get my sneakers?"

"They were in *my* room under the bed," said my mother with a smile on her face.

That's right, I thought as I felt my face getting red. I had just been in there trying to call my friend Paul Thompson. But the line had been busy. My mother dropped my sneaks on the floor and went downstairs.

Ringggg, ringggg. It had to be Paul. I quickly ran into my parents' room and grabbed the phone. My mother picked it up in the kitchen at the same time I answered "Hello" in her bedroom.

"Brechello, is Brrechie there?"

The belching introduction was unmistakable. "Paul, you weirdo! How the hell are you?"

"Brecheffic, brecheffic, brechhhhhhhhhhefic." As Paul paused to catch his breath my mother hung up the phone. "Richie, are you still there?"

"Where do you think I went?" I replied.

"Then who just hung up?" I didn't bother to answer, because I knew Paul would figure it out himself in just a second. "Oh, no," he said with a sudden recognition in his voice. "Tell me it wasn't your mother."

"Okay," I replied, trying to honor his request. "It wasn't my mother."

"No, really, was it? What will she think of me? How can I face her tonight when I come over for dinner?"

"Speaking of dinner, how soon can you come over?"

"Anytime, just tell me when."

"I probably have to do some things around here, so plan to come over around three."

Paul hesitated for a second. "I think I have to do something at three, but any other time would be good."

"So come at four."

"Four would be fine. No, wait, I think I promised my grandmother I'd help her do some shopping, but I should be home no later than five."

"So come at five."

"We're expecting someone from the phone company to fix our phone, and if he hasn't come by then, and if my mother has to do some errands, I'll have to wait for him to come."

"When can you come?" I asked.

"Anytime you say," replied Paul.

"Five forty-five." That was my last offer.

"I'll be there no later than six," he countered.

This was typical Paul. He'd give you the impression he'd do whatever you wanted him to do, but when you told him what it was, he'd have some excuse why he couldn't do it. Sometimes it was very annoying. I guess today, because I hadn't seen him for two months, it didn't matter.

"How was the girl situation up at camp this year?" asked Paul.

"It was okay. There was one cute girl who was dying to go out with me, but I played hard to get the first month. Then I decided to give her a break. So I asked her to go with me on the hayride. Midway through the ride I put my arm around her and pulled her close to me. I looked deeply into her eyes, and would you believe it, they were red and puffy. In fact, her whole face was puffy and covered with red blotches. She really looked gross. I slowly took my arm away from her shoulder and slid away from her. I knew it wasn't possible, but I thought she had leprosy. It turned out to be an allergic reaction to hay. After that she never quite looked the same to me. How about you? Didja see any girls?"

Paul paused. That either meant he hadn't gone out but

was trying to make up a story to cover it up, or he had gone out and was trying to find a way to tell me he hadn't. "I didn't have time for girls this summer," he said. "I was practicing basketball and soccer every day from morning till night. An athlete has to sacrifice something if he wants to be the best. If a girl is really interested in me, she'll just have to wait."

"I agree. If they want us bad enough, they'll have to wait." As I shifted my position, my eye caught the silhouette of my little brother standing in the doorway with a basketball in his hand. His hair was almost in his eyes and his nose was running. I don't know how long he had been standing there, but as far as I was concerned it was already long enough.

"One second, Paul," I said. "What do you want, Robbie?"

"Can I ask you a question?" he said.

I nodded yes.

"Richie, will you play basketball with me today?"

"Maybe when I get off the phone," I replied as I returned to my conversation with Paul. I already knew what was going to happen.

"Richie," interrupted my brother again.

He's so predictable. He always has to ask three questions before he'll be satisfied and leave. "If I'm not in my room when you go out to play, look for me in the basement. Okay?"

"Don't worry, I'll find you," I said in a reassuring tone. "Now, will you let me talk?"

"Okay," he said, but instead of leaving the room he continued staring at me, and to make matters worse, he started to bounce the basketball.

"Richie, are you still there?" asked Paul.

"Hang on, Paul. This will just take one more second." I propped myself up on my elbows and asked Robbie,

"Any more questions?" Robbie nodded his head and in a very low tone asked, "What was the name of the girl with the leprosy you went with on the hayride?"

"None of your business. Now, get out of here!"

"Why?"

My patience was beginning to wear thin. "Because I want to talk in private to Paul."

"Oh," he said slowly, as if it had never occurred to him that this was why I wanted him to leave. "If I'm not in my room I'll be—"

"Basement," I interrupted. "Now, leave right away or I won't play ball with you at all . . . ever."

"Or maybe the kitchen," he yelled back. He always had to get in the last word. The sound of the bouncing ball faded once Robbie got to his room and closed the door.

"Sorry, Paul. Now, where were we? Girls," we both said simultaneously. "I wonder what the new crop of girls will look like," I pondered out loud. The new crop referred to the girls from the other junior high in the area that would join with our class to form the new freshman class in the high school.

"I heard that all the girls in the other junior high are beautiful."

"That's funny," I replied. "My cousin Charlie goes to the other school, and he's always telling me how beautiful he heard the girls in our school are."

"You know the old expression," said Paul with a chuckle in his voice. "The girls are always prettier on the other side of the township."

"Richie, get off the phone," yelled my mom from downstairs.

"Listen, Paul. I have to go. See you at six."

"Five after," said Paul. I could tell he was smiling as he hung up the phone. I was smiling too!

2

After dinner we went up to my room. "The other day my mom was talking about you. She thinks you're so polite, so considerate, so everything."

Hearing that made Paul start to laugh.

"What's so funny?" I asked.

"My mother thinks you're perfect too. Hey, I have a great idea. Since your mother thinks I'm so great and my mother thinks you're so great, maybe we should switch families."

"I always wanted to be an only child. How about if I pack up my things and plan to move to your house tonight?"

"By the way," said Paul, "you have two cars to wash and a redwood table to repaint tomorrow."

"That's okay," I replied. "You have to take my brother and sister to the zoo." We both flopped down on the bed. "Boy, am I stuffed."

"Me too. Your mom is a great cook. My mom is another story. I like to think of her as a very religious cook."

"Religious?" I repeated.

"Yeah, she likes to serve burnt offerings."

"She's not that bad."

"Do you know she cooked a turkey so long the other day, it had to be served in its own cremation urn?"

For a second I almost believed Paul. He always tells me these things with such a straight face. And his expression usually doesn't change until he's sure he's fooled me. *Next time*, I always say to myself, *next time he won't fool me*. But he always does.

"You don't expect me to fall for that, do you?"

"No, you're too smart for me," said Paul.

"What do you want to do tonight?"

"Whatever you want to do," said Paul.

"How about the movies? I'll ask my father if he can drive us."

"Naw, I just went to the movies two days ago. Besides there's nothing good around."

"Do you want to call some girls?"

"Who can we call?"

"How about Mary from across the street?"

"Naw, she's boring."

"Rachel, from math class."

"Forget it."

"Brenda."

"Yecch!"

"Then you pick someone."

"I changed my mind. Let's not call anybody."

"Then what do you want to do?" I said, feeling a little bit exasperated.

"Whatever you want," replied Paul.

I rolled over onto my side and just stared at him in silence. When he realized I hadn't talked for about a minute, he rolled over onto his side on the other bed and started to stare at me. The staring continued for about two more minutes. Finally I got up and, still without saying anything, started to walk over to the record player as if I were going to put on another album. When I got behind the bed Paul was on, I gave out a blood-curdling yell and leaped onto his back. This took him completely by surprise, and by the time he realized what was happening I had him completely wrapped up like a pretzel.

"Give up?" I yelled.

"*Noooooooooo*," yelled Paul as he struggled to get free.

"Give up?" I repeated, applying more pressure to his arms.

"*Never!*"

"What did you say?" I asked again as I applied even more pressure to his arms and now to his legs.

"*Nev*—I give, I give. Now let go."

"Now let's see, that's two hundred thirty-four thousand, five hundred sixty-six wins for me and two hundred thirty-four thousand, five hundred sixty-five wins for—"

"The only way you can beat me is by sneak attack," said Paul, sitting up now as he rubbed his wrists.

"And what about the time right before camp when you asked me to help you carry your mother's packages into the house for you, and when I got into the kitchen you jumped me before I had a chance to put anything down? Huh?"

Paul lay back down on the bed and put his hands behind his head. He cleared his throat as he does all the time before he's going to say, "That was a different story. . . ." or "That time it was a different story because . . ."

"Because you were doing it to me, not vice versa," I replied as I returned to the other bed.

We both looked at each other and laughed. You'd

probably think that with all the fighting and needling and disagreements that went on between us we seemed more like enemies than friends, but the truth of the matter was we had been the best of friends since we were seven years old, and as far as I was concerned, Paul and I would be best of friends for our whole lives. "How about a little B-ball tomorrow?"

"You're on," said Paul without a moment's hesitation. "What time?"

Not this again, I thought. "You tell me," I asked.

"Let's see, Tony said he'd be over at—"

I propped myself up on my elbows and I turned my head toward Paul. "Tony? Who's Tony?"

"Remember at dinner when I told you I wanted to tell you something and you said, 'What is it?' and I started to tell you and your brother knocked the milk all over your sister and she began to yell at him and your father spazzed out and told everyone to be quiet?" I nodded my head. "Well, by the time we could talk again, I forgot what I was going to tell you. But now I remember. It was about Tony."

"Tony who?" I repeated again, still puzzled as to who or what Tony was.

"He's a new kid who moved into the neighborhood while you were at camp."

"Where does he live?"

"You know that big house on the corner of Second and Parker?"

"The house with the pool in the backyard?"

"That's the one. Behind the trees on the other side of the house is a paved area for half-court basketball."

"Sounds like he's rich," I said.

"He doesn't act like a rich kid," said Paul. "You're going to like him. I just know it."

"How did you meet him?" I asked.

"Oh, I don't know. It happened one day. I was shooting baskets at my house and Tony was just walking by and he asked me if he could play. We shot around for a while and then I challenged him to a game of twenty-one. My court, my basket, my ball, no contest, right? *Wrong!* He beat me twenty-one to nothing. That's because I let him go first. When I went first I only lost by nine, twenty-one to twelve. He's got some shot. I'll introduce you to him tomorrow."

"Sounds like fun," I replied. "Now, what are we going to do the rest of the night?"

"I just got a great idea," said Paul. "How about going to the movies? Why don't you ask your father if he can take us?"

I got up from the bed without saying a word and unlocked my door. *"Dad,"* I yelled at the top of my lungs. *"Can you take Paul and me to the movies?"* Silence. I was just about to repeat myself when a reply came from the direction of the den.

"What time is the show?"

"Seven-thirty," I yelled back.

"Be ready in ten minutes," he replied.

I was about to tell Paul he had to get up when I felt both his hands around my waist. The next thing I knew, Paul was on top of me.

"Give up?"

"Hey, look, Paul," I said in a very controlled voice, "we have to get ready to go."

"Give up?"

"We have to get ready to go to the movies," I said again in a louder voice. "Besides, this time doesn't count."

"I'm not letting go until you give up, movie or no movie."

"I'm not giving up," I said. *I can be as stubborn as you,* I thought. Paul tightened his grip. "Give up, give up."

"Are you guys going or not?" My father was standing in the doorway with his hands on his hips. Paul looked at me and I looked at him. He loosened his grip and I wriggled free.

"I really won," said Paul.

"If we didn't have to leave, I would have gotten free on my own in another minute."

"Sure, sure," he said. My father shook his head as he watched us continue going back and forth on our way downstairs. We continued all the way to the movies. We started again on the way home. And the last thing Paul said to me before he went to sleep was "I won."

"Okay," I said, wanting to get some sleep. "You won." I figured I'd give him this one. Tomorrow I'd get him when he was brushing his teeth.

3

It was after twelve when we finished one of my mother's fantastic pancake breakfasts and started out for Paul's house.

"Did you remember to bring a bathing suit?" asked Paul when we arrived at his house.

"You never said anything about bringing a suit."

"Don't worry about it, Richie. If we do go swimming, you can use your shorts." When Paul went into the house to get his stuff, I grabbed a basketball from his garage and began to shoot around. I threw up a couple of jump shots just to get the feel of the basket, and then I settled myself on the foul line. I had a streak going of eighteen in a row when Paul came outside.

Paul always gets a very smug look on his face before he says something he knows will tick me off. "You'd better practice," he said, "because I think Tony's going to whip you badly."

"Just because he can beat you easily doesn't mean he'll have the same luck with me." I resumed my foul shooting only to have my next shot hit the front rim and bounce away.

"Sure, sure," said Paul. "Come on, let's go."

Tony's house was a short walk from Paul's. As we approached, we could hear the sound of a bouncing basketball coming from behind a thick hedge. "About halfway down there's a break in the hedge," said Paul, motioning with his left hand.

I followed Paul's finger to where there should have been an opening, but it wasn't until we were both almost on top of it that I saw it. Paul nodded for me to go first, but I declined and followed him onto the court. Tony paused for a second as he heard us arrive, but instead of coming over to greet us, he continued shooting from all over the court until he missed. He was about my height, but his skinny, wiry frame made him look a little taller. He retrieved his missed shot and threw a pass to Paul. Then he looked in my direction and smiled.

"Tony, I'd like you to meet Richie. Richie—Tony," said Paul.

I knocked the ball out of Paul's hand and dribbled toward Tony. Just before I got to him I let one fly from the foul line. Swish. I smiled a triumphant smile and extended my hand to Tony.

"Paul's told me a lot about you," said Tony as we shook.

"I wouldn't believe a word Paul says," I replied, trying to be funny.

Tony smiled a polite smile and moved to retrieve the ball. For a split second Tony looked in my direction and then, turning in one graceful motion, he put up a jump shot that only hit net. Smoothly he got his own rebound and probably would have continued to shoot if Paul hadn't yelled for the ball.

"Want something to drink?" asked Tony. I shook my

head no and Paul followed suit. "I'm going to go in and get some water," said Tony. "I'll be right out."

I followed Tony with my eyes until he'd disappeared through another break in a far hedge at the back end of the court. Beyond the hedge you could see the upper two thirds of a gigantic old three-story house. To the left of the opening Tony had gone out was another opening, and through this, one could barely make out the outline of a pool.

"It's some house, isn't it?" said Paul.

"You can say that again," I replied. "What does his father do besides make money?" Paul shrugged his shoulders and passed the ball to me. Out of the corner of my eye I saw Tony returning. I took two short dribbles with the ball and let a long jumper fly from just behind the circle. Swish. I got my own rebound and started to shoot my famous fadeaway hook shot when Paul sneaked up behind me and knocked the ball out of my hand. "You turkey, Paul!" I yelled as I turned to run after him, but instead I found myself face to face with Tony.

"He's such a turkey sometimes," I said.

"Yeah, I know what you mean," said Tony.

This time I gave him a more careful look. He wasn't as tall as I had originally thought, nor as muscular. "Where did you move from?" I asked.

"Detroit," said Tony, putting up another shot. It missed.

"Why did you move here?" I asked, tipping in the rebound.

"My father owns a computer consulting firm and he just moved his main offices here."

Boy, I never knew you could make so much money in computers, I thought to myself. *Maybe I'll be a computer consultant instead of a dentist.* "Have any brothers or sisters?"

"Yeah, one nuisance of a sister. And you?"

"One of each."

A moment of awkward silence followed. *He really doesn't look like a bad kid. We'll find out soon enough. I like the way he shoots his jump shots. Maybe he'll teach me how. I could probably teach him a few things. If he's lucky, maybe I will.*

"Are you guys going to talk all day, or can we play something?"

"I haven't even warmed up yet."

"You mean a great star like you has to practice?"

I gave Paul my sit-on-it look and began to take shots from all over the court. Even though he wasn't making it obvious, I could tell that Tony was watching my every move.

"Come on, Richie. We don't have all day." said Paul.

"Hold your horses. I just want to shoot a couple fouls."

"Okay, just five and then let's play pig."

"How about pest," I said as I canned the fifth foul.

"Very funny. I'll beat you both at either."

So pest it was, with Paul first, me second, and Tony third. Five turns later Paul was out of the game and Tony and I were battling it out. We were evenly matched, and after we'd traded makes and misses, it was all even at PES apiece. It was my turn, and all I had to do was make my famous fadeaway hook and the game was mine. The worst thing you can do in a situation like this is to start to think about what you are going to do, because when you do, you screw up. Think about it. What happens when you think about how you're walking? You trip. Or when you think about carrying a cup of hot coffee? You spill it. Or what you are going to say when you introduce someone to somebody else? You get mixed up. Somewhere in one of those fortune cookies it probably says Don't think before you take an important shot today! Unfortunately, I thought and missed. Tony put in his next shot, and dummy that I am, I thought again, and this time it cost me the game. *Darn it. I could have beaten him. Maybe next time!*

"I told you he was good," said Paul with a smug look on his face. I tried not to show how mad I was. Not at Tony for winning, but at me for losing.

"Let's play twenty-one," said Tony.

The inevitable twenty-one game, I thought.

"I'm first," insisted Paul. He took the ball from Tony and approached the foul line. Paul ran off eleven points and then blew an easy lay-up. Kicking the ground in disgust, he started to hand me the ball. "You're next," he said.

All of a sudden this didn't seem like a game anymore. It was as if I had to prove something to Tony, to Paul, to myself. "No, that's okay," I said, and handed the ball to Tony. "I'll go last."

Tony took the ball and went to the foul line. I watched him closely to see if I could pick up some of his secrets. For every shot he did the same thing. First he picked up his pants and then he bent down and straightened out his cuffs. Next he bounced the ball five times, paused, bounced it two times more, took a deep breath, looked down at the ground then up quickly at the basket, another pause, and then shot. Swish, lay-up . . . three. Swish, lay-up . . . six . . . nine . . . twelve . . . fifteen . . . twenty-one . . . *I've got nothing else to do today* . . . twenty-four . . . *Maybe I'll have dinner* . . . twenty-seven . . . *Maybe I'll come back after breakfast* . . . twenty-nine . . . *He missed a little jump shot. He's human. He can miss.*

"Your turn, Richie. Didn't I tell you he was good?"

If you tell me that one more time I'm going to stick this basketball up your . . . I thought but didn't say. *Well, I might as well get this game over. At least I can beat Paul.* Swish, lay-up . . . three . . . swish, lay-up. *Six, nine, twelve, fifteen. What a touch* . . . eighteen . . . twenty-one . . . *I'm cooking* . . . twenty-four . . . *Maybe I can beat Tony* . . . twenty-seven . . . *Don't think* . . . *Concentrate* . . . *is that thinking?* . . . *no, don't concentrate. Just do what you did before. What was I doing before? I can't remember. Was it two dribbles or three? You're thinking? Stop it. Okay I'll stop. How can you turn your mind off? Just shoot! Okay.* SWISH. TWENTY-NINE. *Just make this lay-up and you've won. It's up. Bouncing on the back of the rim, rolling around, bouncing again and* . . . *everything's in slow motion. The shot is* . . . good.

It's good. Thirty. *I win. It's good.*

"See, I told you he was good," said Paul to Tony.

"Great shooting," said Tony. He patted me on the back.

"Didn't I tell you he was a natural shooter? He's so relaxed and confident on the line. Nothing bothers him."

I looked at Paul and then at Tony. I would never disagree with the truth.

"How would you guys like to take a swim?" said Tony. "No, wait," he said before we had a chance to reply. "Nobody's home right now. That means we can only use the spa. Let me run ahead and turn things on." Tony disappeared in an instant. There were so many different hedge entrances and exits that this place was beginning to look like the queen's palace in *Alice in Wonderland.*

Paul could tell from the expression on my face that I didn't know what to do next, so he motioned for me to follow him through the left opening in the hedge. Beyond was a very large kidney-shaped pool with a diving board at one end. Behind the diving board was a big circle of trees. As we approached the trees, we could hear a bubbling sound. "The spa's in there," said Paul. Paul held back a tree for me, and I peeked in. There was a three-foot-wide plot of grass which ran around the outside. The spa itself looked like a very fancy tiled kiddies' pool. "Go in," said Paul, nudging me from the back. "The steps are over there."

I sat down on the grass and took off my sneaks and socks. "Take everything off," said Tony as he appeared from the other side. "Nobody can see in here, and besides, my mother and sister won't be back for a couple of hours." I looked over at Paul. He must have done this before, because he already had his suit off. Tony was not far behind, so I took off the rest of my clothes and threw them in a pile under one of the trees and got in.

The water already in the spa was cool, but the water coming in through the five jets spaced around was boiling hot. Tony explained that all the water was recirculated through the heater, and in about thirty minutes all the water would be as hot as the water from the jets. The spa itself was about three feet deep, but at one and a half feet a ledge came out and around for you to sit on. We placed ourselves each in front of our own jet, closed our eyes, and leaned back to soak up the rays.

I could feel the water getting warmer, and I probably would have fallen asleep if I hadn't heard what sounded like female voices. "What's that?"

Paul looked at Tony as if he already knew the answer and then yelled, "Oh, no, it's your mom!"

Paul was only partially right. It was his sister and mom. My hands went under the water to cover myself up.

"Hi, Paul," said Tony's mother. Paul nodded his head and smiled back.

"Mom, I want you to meet Richie," said Tony.

I nodded my head and smiled, too, but Tony's mother came over to the edge of the spa and extended her hand. I instinctively started to get up, extending my own hand,

but quickly slid under the water again. This forced Tony's mother to stoop down in order to shake my hand. As
we made contact the smile seemed to broaden on her
face. "Nice to meet you, Richie," she said.

"Nice to meet you too," I replied. My ears were burn-
ing hot. If they got any hotter I was sure they would turn
to ashes and fall off my head.

"Where do you live?" she asked.

I withdrew my hand and slid it under the water. *Now I
don't think she can see anything at all.* "Over on Hawthorne
Place," I replied. She got up, and just as I was about to
breathe a sigh of relief, she motioned for Tony's sister,
who had remained by the bushes, to come over. I could
feel Tony's sister's eyes penetrating the water as she got
closer. I felt like standing up on the seat and yelling,
"Take a good look. Satisfied? It's just like your brother's."
But instead I sank farther into the water.

"This is Susie," said Tony's mother. We stared at each
other in silence. I finally was able to force out a "Hi" as I
floated to the opposite side. "Susie and I are going to go
in and get our suits on, and then you all can go in the big
pool," said Tony's mother as they left.

As soon as they disappeared I got out of the spa and
made a beeline for my clothes. Paul and Tony were not
far behind. "You can't see into the spa when you're standing up," reassured Tony.

"Are you sure?" I asked.

"Positive, and I'll prove it," said Tony. He went into the
main pool area and returned with a horseshoe. He tossed
it into the spa. "When it hits the bottom you won't even
know it's there," said Tony.

Paul and I followed the horseshoe's path as it sank to
the bottom. Not only could we see it clearly on the bottom, but we could even make out the word CHAMPIONSHIP

written on it. Paul looked at me and I looked at him, and then the two of us took off after Tony. "Honest, guys, I really thought you couldn't see, honest." When we caught up with him, we dragged him over to the edge of the pool and waited for his mother to return before we threw him in. I fully expected Tony's mother to ask who I was, and when Tony introduced me again she would say, "Oh, I didn't recognize you with your clothes on." But that never happened.

At the end of the day I had to walk home alone because Tony had invited Paul to sleep over. I sort of hoped that he would invite me over, too, but he didn't. I really didn't think much about it on the way home or during dinner or when I was watching TV. It didn't bother me. Why should it? Tony didn't even know me yet. Paul was still my best friend. My head hit the pillow at eleven. I couldn't sleep.

4

I called Paul late the next afternoon, but he still wasn't home from Tony's. I waited until after dinner to call again. "Hi, Mrs. Thompson. Is Paul there?"

"He's in the shower now, but I'll have him call you when he gets out."

"Thanks," I replied, and hung up. I sat by the phone, expecting him to call back right away, but after about ten minutes I gave up and went in to watch TV. He was probably taking a long shower. It was no big deal. I knew he would call back soon. When he hadn't called back by nine, I was beginning to get a little angry. Maybe his mother hadn't given him the message. That was certainly possible, but unlikely. Maybe he'd had to go out with his parents and hadn't had time to call back. That must be why he'd been taking a shower. He'd probably gone over to his aunt's house. *I know what I'll do. I'll call one more time. If there's no answer, then he's at his aunt's. But if Paul answers, well, first I'll ask him if he got my message and then . . . I* dialed Paul's number and it rang two times before his father picked it up.

"Hello."

I was so mad I didn't know what to say. "Hello, hello."

If he wants to speak to me, he'll just have to call me. And with that I slammed down the phone.

Paul finally called the next night during dinner. "Where have you been?" he asked. "I've been trying to reach you all afternoon."

"I was here," I replied in a very nonchalant tone. "I was outside shooting baskets. If you had called me back last night, you would have known where to find me."

"I never got a message that you called, and besides I did try to reach you," said Paul in a somewhat annoyed tone.

"Listen, I have to finish my dinner. I'll call you back when I'm done."

"I won't be home later."

"How come?"

"Don't you remember I told you that I was leaving for the seashore tonight? We're going for two weeks this year instead of one, so I'll be back the day before school starts."

"Oh," I said in a disappointed tone. "Have a nice time."

"I'll call you when I get back."

"Yeah, fine," I said, before hanging up the phone. I didn't eat any more dinner that night.

Paul was true to his word this time, for he called me the night before school started, just as he'd promised.

"When did you get home?" I asked, anxious to hear about his vacation.

"About an hour ago," said Paul.

"How was the shore?" I asked.

"I was just telling Tony how great it was this year.

There was this one girl who was really put together, and she used to wear these incredible bikini bathing suits that almost covered her. Well, one day I was body surfing and so was she, and we accidentally bumped into each other. We started talking and, well, one thing led to another, and I'll leave the rest to your imagination."

"What happened?" I asked, pressing Paul for an answer.

"Well, you know."

"Did you really?"

"I wouldn't lie to you, now, would I?"

I'd known Paul long enough to know that "I wouldn't lie to you, now" meant that Paul had hardly talked to the girl, if there ever had been a girl to begin with. It wasn't that Paul really lied. He just stretched the truth. "You're incredible. Did you get her number?"

"I forgot to."

"You forgot?" I said in a loud voice, almost yelling into the phone. "How could you forget?"

"I just forgot."

"Well, what was her name?" I asked. Now I was really putting the screws to him.

"Her first name was . . . uh, Amy, and her last name was . . . I forget."

"You can't even remember her last name?"

"I think it began with an *S*, but I'm not sure."

"How could you forget?" I repeated again.

"I just forgot," said Paul again. "Now, will you get off my case? Besides, I have to get off the phone now. I'll see you on the bus tomorrow."

"Save me a seat," I said.

Most of the time I pretend to believe him. Tonight I didn't feel like doing that.

*   *   *

Nobody in his right mind looks forward to the first day of school or the second or the third or the . . . But this year I was a little excited to begin for one reason. I was in ninth grade, the first year of high school, and I was going to a new school.

My alarm woke me at six-thirty, and as I peered at the sun creeping around the corners of my shade, I knew summer was over.

"Richie, get up!"

"I am up!"

"Get out of bed."

I reached over the side of the bed and picked up my shoes. I raised them high above my head and dropped them onto the floor. That should keep my mom quiet for a while. I put my hands behind my head and closed my eyes for a few extra *zzzz*'s. I don't know if I fell asleep or just had a daydream. I saw myself in school surrounded by five of the prettiest girls from the other junior high. I looked at each one very carefully. I wanted to be sure I picked the best. I was just about to choose a dynamite blonde when a girl came up behind me and started to tap me on the shoulder. When I didn't pay any attention to her, she began to tap me harder, and then she started to tug at my arm. "Get out of here," I yelled, pulling my arm away.

"Richie, get up. You'll be late!"

"I am up. I am up," I said, and slowly opened my eyes. "Oh, hi, Mom. I was just getting out of bed." My mother waited till I'd sat up and had both feet on the floor before she disappeared downstairs. I did ten deep knee-bends in an effort to wake myself up a little bit more, and then staggered down the hall to the bathroom, where I brushed my teeth. I went back to my room to finish dressing, then walked downstairs. My mother had prepared the first-day breakfast banquet.

"I only want juice."

"That's not enough. Eat some cereal."

"I don't want cereal. I'll take a piece of toast and eat it on the way to the bus stop."

"Richie, toast is not enough. You need—"

"So long, Mom. We have our physicals for soccer after school, so I'll come home on the sports bus."

"Richie, you need . . ." I think my mother yelled something else to me from the kitchen door just as I was turning the corner, but I didn't bother to look back.

It was a beautiful morning, certainly too nice to waste in school. I don't know why I turned around when I did. Maybe it was instinct or maybe I heard footsteps, but nevertheless I did and there, about a hundred yards behind me, was Chuck. Chuck was a kid who'd gone to my camp—not this year, but last year. And I'd sort of lost track of him. You see, Chuck is a real turkey, or he used to be a real turkey. You could just look at him and tell he was one by the way he walked or dressed. For some reason, today he looked different, and for the life of me I couldn't tell why. When he saw me turn around he waved, and I returned the gesture but kept walking. I wanted to turn around and look again to see if I could find out what the difference was, but I didn't.

There were already ten kids, all upperclassmen, at the bus stop when I arrived, so I stood off to the side by myself to wait for the bus. As luck would have it, Chuck joined me, and putting his notebooks on the ground, he said in a low voice, "Hi."

I nodded my head.

"Notice anything new about me?" he asked.

I glanced at him quickly and shook my head.

He pointed to his eyes and said, "My glasses are gone. Contacts."

Without glasses Chuck looked almost human. In fact, he really looked great. He even looked a little taller too. "I almost didn't recognize you. Have you gotten taller?"

"I grew two inches over the summer—and," said Chuck, pausing just enough to give what he was to say next its proper emphasis, "I lost twenty pounds."

"Twenty pounds!"

Chuck nodded his head.

I made a gesture with my hand indicating he looked okay, and Chuck responded with a big smile. I don't know if I would have talked more to Chuck or he to me, but just then the bus arrived, and without hesitation I pushed my way into the crowd, leaving him standing there all alone. Once on the bus I saw Paul motioning me to come back to a seat he had saved between himself and Tony.

Paul tugged my sleeve as I sat down. "That isn't Chuck, is it?"

I nodded and Tony asked, "Who's Chuck?"

"Some kid who lives in the neighborhood," I replied.

"Boy, does he look different," said Paul. "I wonder if he acts different."

"How did he act before?" asked Tony.

"He used to look and act like a nerd," said Paul.

I wanted to say, "Maybe he's different now," but instead I said, "Yeah, he was a turkey all right."

"Listen," said Paul, changing the subject, "I told Tony that we would have time to give him a tour of the school before we have to report to homeroom."

"How can we give him a tour of a school we never attended before?" I asked.

"Leave that to me," said Paul. "We can start at the

lunchroom, work our way over to the girls' locker room, and then, if we have time, show him where the class-rooms are."

"We'd better show him where to get the bus home also, since we both have to stay after to get our physicals for soccer."

"That won't be necessary, Richie," said Paul. "Tony is playing soccer, too, so he'll be with us."

"Tony plays soccer too?" I said in a surprised tone. Paul seemed to ignore my question—not that it needed any answer—and he started talking again about this great tour he had planned for Tony. I got very quiet and I started staring up at the ceiling of the bus. The bus was very old and the paint was chipped off in many places. One area over by the door caught my eye. The paint must have been off quite a long time, and one of the bare spots had rusted, causing it to look like a face with a black eye.

The next thing I knew, Paul was trying to climb over me to get to the aisle. "Can't you wait a second?" I snapped.

"I asked you three times to go, but you were too busy staring up into space," replied Paul.

I think I purposely got up slowly now, and I didn't rush, either, to get off the bus. Paul gave me a what's-eating-you look when he got off.

"I think I'll skip the tour," I said. "I'll see you guys at the nurse's office."

"What about lunch?" asked Tony.

"Oh, yeah, I forgot. See you at lunch," I said on the way to my homeroom. I think I heard Paul say to Tony, "What's with him?" and Tony replying, "Oh, what's the difference?"

5

I don't know why the teachers try to teach us anything on the first day. They should break us in slowly. Don't they know our brains are still rusty? And to make matters worse, biology class was right before lunch, and that was bad, because when I'm hungry I can't concentrate. In fact, the only thing I could seem to concentrate on was a girl sitting two rows in front of me and to my left. I think she liked me, because every few minutes she'd look back over her shoulder at me, and the last time she gave me a big smile. *There, she just did it again. Only ten more minutes until lunch. What's she talking about now? Mitosis? Mioses? Mistomach! That's the only mi I'm interested in. I wonder who that girl is? I've never seen her before, so she must have gone to the other school. I think I'm in love.* This time she pretended to drop her pencil, but I saw her look back. When the bell rang I'd get her name and phone number and then I'd . . .

Ring! Ring! I'd thought the period would never end. I stood up and watched the mystery beauty come down the aisle toward my desk. My words had to be precise and to the point. My timing had to be just right.

"Could you give me the pages we have to read for tomorrow again?" asked Paul.

"Wait a second." She was almost here.

"The kid in front of me sneezed just as she was giving out the pages and I didn't—"

"Can you hold your horses for a second?"

"Just say if it begins on page fifteen or sixteen and I'll figure out the rest."

I turned my head just for a second to say, "Fifteen! Fifteen! Fifteen," and she was gone. "Do you see what you just made me do?"

"What?" said Paul in a very puzzled tone.

"You just made me miss getting the phone number of that girl. Now I have to wait until tomorrow."

"What girl?"

"Forget it."

"I think you'll live," said Paul. "Besides, eating is more important than girls right now." As we walked to the lunchroom I tried to think of something to say in disagreement with his last statement, but I couldn't. On the way in I stopped to read the menu posted on the cafeteria door.

BAKED VIRGINIA
TUNA PLATTER
COOKIES
JELL-O
MILK
ICE CREAM
SOFT PRETZELS

I waved to Paul to save me a seat and then got into the lunch line. I sort of remembered that we had had tuna platters and baked Virginia for lunch the last day of school before it closed for the summer. Not only had they saved the food from last June, but they'd even brought it over to the high school for us. That thought made me nauseous.

"Tuna or baked Virginia?"

The tuna looked green and the baked Virginia looked petrified. "Nothing for me," I said, and grabbed a soft pretzel and milk instead. The lady behind the counter mumbled something under her breath as she began to serve the person behind me.

"Do you remember what we had for lunch the last day before the summer?" I asked, sitting down at the table with Paul and Tony.

"Hot dogs and P and J," said Tony.

"Very funny. I mean here, dummy." I had turned to look at Paul.

"I don't remember," he said.

"Think. It's important."

"Baked Virginia and tuna. Happy now?"

"I knew it. I knew it. They froze the leftovers." I cupped my hand around my mouth and pretended to make an announcement. "Now hear this. Now hear this. The food you are eating is two months old. The food you are eating is—"

Paul tapped me on the shoulder. "Three tables are staring at us. Shhh."

I covered my face with my hands and slid down in my chair. "Is it safe to come out?" I asked.

"Get a load of that table," said Paul.

I took my hands away from my face. "Where?"

"Over there," said Paul pointing over my shoulder. "The table with the blonde."

I turned and looked in the direction he was pointing. "I don't see any blonde."

"Over there." He turned my head slightly to the left.

"I still don't see where you . . . oh, my God. I think I'm in love."

"I saw her first," said Paul. "She's mine!"

"Why don't you go over and introduce yourself to her?" I asked.

"I'm in the middle of lunch," said Paul. "I'll go over when I finish."

Tony looked at me as I turned to look at him. We traded sure-sure looks and then turned them toward Paul. "Honest, guys. You wait and see. As soon as I finish this half of my sandwich, I'll be off to sweep her off her feet."

I returned to eating my pretzel and looking over the new crop when my eyes came to rest on a truly unbelievable sight. "Am I awake? Pinch me. I must be dreaming. Check out the two babes eating lunch with Chuck. One of them is that fox from biology."

"I got the tall one," said Tony.

"I guess that leaves the short one for me," said Paul.

"I saw them first, guys," I chimed in. "So don't get any ideas."

"You can't go out with both," said Tony.

"Why not? One for the weekdays and one for the weekend," I replied.

"If you had to pick one, which would you pick?" asked Tony.

I looked at both girls closely before answering. The tall one, the one from biology class, was really beautiful. She had beautiful brown hair, and a really infectious smile. The other one was not bad either. A little on the skinny side, perhaps, and not as well built, but acceptable.

She looked like the quieter one and would probably be harder to talk to the first time. You know, the yes-no-maybe-I-don't-know kind on the phone. The choice was easy, and I was about to say the tall one when Tony said, "Okay, Mr. Macho, you finished your sandwich. Now it's time to introduce yourself to the blonde."

"I want to have a soft pretzel first. Then I'll go over," said Paul.

"And after the pretzel he'll have another milk and then a soda and then a baked—"

"No, really, guys. I promise. After this pretzel I'm going over." Paul didn't wait for Tony's or my comment. Instead he headed toward the pretzel counter and came back with three pretzels.

I was just about to remind Paul that he'd said "*a* pretzel," when he gave one to me and one to Tony. Shortly afterward I turned back to look at the table Chuck and the two girls had been sitting at—but now it was empty. "Finish your pretzel yet?" I asked. I'd been staring at Paul's every bite.

"Will you guys cut it out? You're making me nervous. I'm eating as fast as I can. Really, I can't eat any faster. If I do I'll choke and then I'll die, and then I won't be able to meet that girl. Look—see?" he said, holding up the last remaining piece of pretzel. "This is it. The last piece and then I'm on my way."

Ringgggggggg. Ringgggggggg.

"Isn't that the bell, guys?"

Tony and I continued to stare at Paul in silence.

"Honest, guys. I was going to go. The clock is fast. There is really five minutes left. With five minutes I could have gone over, swept her off her feet, and given her my number so she could call me tonight."

"Sure, sure," said the two of us in unison.

"I'm going to the office right now to tell them the school clock is fast. For all the money my parents pay in taxes, you would think they'd have a clock that worked properly," said Paul on his way out of the lunchroom.

"See you at the nurse's office after school," Tony reminded me as he left.

"See you then," I yelled back halfheartedly. I went off to my locker to get my books.

Boy, do I hate physicals at school. I don't mind the beginning, when the doctor looks in your ears and listens to your chest. The part I hate comes at the end, when you drop your pants and cough. And that wouldn't be so bad if the school nurse weren't around staring at you. My parents called them "private parts" once when I was three, and I think they should be private parts from the nurse too. But no matter how you angle your body or cross your legs, the nurse manages to get a good look at you.

I think most nurses are sex maniacs anyway. My friend told me a story about a nurse at camp who used to paint all the boys' crotches who had jock rash with this red medicine that burned. She painted so many crotches one summer, we gave her the nickname "Picasso." One day this kid went into the infirmary to get an allergy shot and before he had a chance to say a word, Picasso told him to go into the back room and drop his pants. "I'm only here for a—"

"Yeah, I know," she says. "Now, get in the back and drop your pants."

"But—"

"No buts, drop your pants."

So the kid went into the next room and got his crotch painted. Afterward Picasso said, "That wasn't so bad, was it?"

To which the kid replied, "I only came here to get my allergy shot."

See what I mean, they're all sex maniacs. Nevertheless, I had to show up if I wanted to play on the team, so as soon as the last period was over I ran right down to the nurse's office. The line began in her outer office and had already overflowed into the hali. I found Tony and Paul inside, and they let me get in behind them.

"I heard that the nurse that works here is just out of school," said Paul.

I looked at Paul closely. He usually gets a funny look on his face when he's not telling the truth. "Who told you that?" I asked.

"I overheard one of the kids in my math class talking about it. He said she was pretty too."

Paul's face looked like he was serious. But that's when I usually get fooled. "I think you're putting me on," I said, trying to call his bluff. I looked over at Tony to see if he might be in on it. If he was, he did a good job of hiding it.

"Don't believe me, then," said Paul. "You'll see soon enough."

"*Next,*" said a voice from the inner office. Paul put his hands across the crotch of his pants and limped into the next room.

"Did I overhear you say that the nurse was young and beautiful?"

There was Chuck standing two places behind us.

"That's what Paul said," I answered. "What sport are you going out for?"

"Soccer," said Chuck. "This is the first time I ever went out for any sport, and to tell you the truth, I'm a little nervous."

"I remember the first time I went out for a sport. I was

nervous too." Tony extended his hand to Chuck. "By the way, my name is Tony."

Chuck seemed taken aback at the introduction, and at first he didn't seem to know what to do. I guess a former turkey isn't used to people being nice to him. "My name is Chuck," he said, and shook Tony's hand.

Just then Paul burst out of the next room. "Wait until you see that nurse. Not only is she pretty, but umm." He made motions with both hands to show her measurements.

"Next!"

Tony walked in backward with one hand covering the front of his pants and the other the back.

"How was it?" I asked.

"Was she really that big?" asked Chuck.

"She was, and it was awful," said Paul, answering both questions at once. "You have to get completely undressed."

"Undressed? Why?"

"So the nurse could get your correct weight."

"Oh," I said. That made sense to me. For once in his life Paul was telling the truth.

"When you were standing there and the nurse was looking at you, how did you stop yourself from getting a . . . ?"

"That's easy, Chuck," interrupted Paul. "Just think of something that has nothing to do with girls or sex. Like sports, farm animals, electrical equipment."

"Next!"

"Paul, you were wrong," said Tony as he emerged from the other room. "She was so big she was almost falling out of her dress."

Behind me I could hear Chuck practicing Paul's suggestion. "Washington Redskins, pigs, light bulbs . . ."

"Wait for me," I said. "I'll be right out." I didn't even bother to cover my pants at all. Once inside, I saw the doctor sitting at a desk writing something. "Take off your shoes and get on the scale," he said.

"Don't you want me to get undressed?" I asked.

"Nope," said the doctor as he continued to write.

While taking off my shoes, I looked around for the nurse. She was nowhere to be found. Perhaps she'd gone out for a drink of water. The doctor got up from his chair and measured my height and weight.

"This may be cold," said the doctor as he placed the head of the stethoscope on my chest and listened to my heart. "Any allergies?"

"No." I thought I heard a sound behind me. I turned. The room was still empty. She was going to jump out any minute now.

"Heart problems?"

"No." *You enjoy torturing me like this, don't you, Nurse?*

"Stomach problems?"

"No." *I guess you're waiting until I drop my pants before you show your face?*

"Taking any medicine?"

"No."

"Okay, drop your pants and drawers to your knees." The doctor went back to his desk and took a rubber glove from the lower drawer and put it on.

I unbuttoned my pants and dropped them to my knees. *I know she's going to come in now,* I thought as I lowered my underpants. *Okay, I'm naked now. Come in. Show time.* I closed my eyes. *You may want to see me, but I don't want to see you.*

"Cough," said the doctor.

I coughed. "Again."

I did it once more.

"That's it. Get dressed."

I was still looking around as I got dressed. Still no nurse. Maybe she'd gotten sick. "Where's the nurse?"

The doctor was already back at his desk writing. He looked up at me and said, "Wish I had one. I'm all the school could afford. A nurse sure would help."

I looked around the room once more, still expecting a nurse to appear. I had been had. I walked out the door and looked around for Tony and Paul. As I walked past Chuck he was still repeating, "Philadelphia Eagles, Guernsey cows, hundred-watt bulbs . . ." I spotted them leaning against the lockers across the hall, laughing hysterically. This time I motioned to them with my hands, but I was not showing measurements. They turned and ran as I chased them down the hall.

6

The soccer team's first practice was two days after the physicals. I don't know if I got there a little late or if Paul and Tony got there early, but they were almost dressed by the time I arrived.

"What's up?" I asked as I started to change.

"Nothing much," said Paul. They started to leave.

"Save me a seat on the bleachers," I yelled. Both Tony and Paul nodded yes as they disappeared around the corner. I have a habit of whistling to pass the time when I'm by myself and that's exactly what I was doing when a familiar voice interrupted me from behind.

"Hey, Richie. Want to come over my house sometime and see my new snake?"

"Your what?"

"My snake," repeated Chuck. "He's really neat looking."

Most people have dogs or cats. It would take someone like Chuck to have a snake.

"I'm allergic to dog and cat hair and I wanted a pet, so I asked for a snake and got one."

"What's his name?" I asked, trying to be funny.

"Julius," said Chuck very seriously.

What should I say next? *That's a very nice name or what tricks can he do or* . . . I couldn't believe I was even involved in a conversation about snakes. "That's great, terrific, great."

"Can you come over this weekend and see Julius?"

"Not this weekend, but maybe another one," I replied, not wanting to hurt his feelings.

"I'm a little nervous about playing soccer. It's mostly my parents' idea to go out for a sport."

"Have you ever played soccer before?" I asked, feeling a little sorry for him. My parents usually told me I was playing sports too much.

"I know all the rules and I've kicked a ball around a little, but I never played in a game."

"Oh," I said, not quite knowing what else to say. Chuck waited till I'd finished tying my shoes, and we walked out together. "By the way, who were those girls you were eating lunch with today?"

Chuck wrinkled his forehead. "Eat lunch . . . uhh . . ."

"I wasn't paying too much attention to them, but I think one had brown hair and was wearing a purple blouse with little boats on it and a tan skirt. The other one was—"

"Oh, those girls," said Chuck with a smile on his face. "They're my sisters."

"Sisters? I didn't know you had any sisters."

"They're not really my sisters. I just call them that. Their parents, the Phillipses, are very good friends with my parents, and we grew up together. They call me their brother."

I didn't want to seem overly interested, even though I was, so I just nodded my head and hoped that Chuck would continue. "They're twins, but you'd never know it, because they're not identical. The shorter one's name is Jill and the taller one's is Ellen."

"The taller one's name is . . ."

"Ellen. She's really nice. How about if I introduce them to you at lunch tomorrow?"

"Yeah, sure, okay," I replied. By this time we had reached the bleachers, and I spotted Paul and Tony with room for only one beside them. "Lunch tomorrow will be fine," I said as I left him to join my friends. Chuck looked around for a moment and then sat himself down in the front row just at the outer edge of the group.

"What was that all about?" asked Tony.

"Remember those cute girls we saw sitting with Chuck in the lunchroom? Well, it turns out—"

"I guess I know what you're having for dessert tomorrow for lunch," joked Tony.

"Remember, too much sweet stuff will make you hyperactive," said Paul.

"Listen, if you take the tall one, I want the short one," said Tony.

"But," said Paul, "if you take the short one, I want the tall one."

A hush came over the group as Coach Johnson approached the stands. He cleared his throat three times, looking us over. He looked about five foot seven and was solid, especially in his legs. Somehow the patches of gray hair that showed through the top of his yellow visor didn't seem to go with his young-looking face. "Everyone who comes to practice and works hard will be on the team," he bellowed in a deep, raspy voice. "Those who work the hardest will play the most. Soccer is a team game. If you want to be a star, maybe you belong over there," he said, and pointed to the football field. "Form five lines and we'll do some warm-up exercises and drills first. Okay, let's go."

Everyone piled out of the stands and into place, and for the next forty-five minutes we stretched and pulled and bent and folded ourselves into positions I'd have thought were only possible if you were a pretzel. After that the coach divided us into two groups and we lined up across the field. The people who were trying out for goalie kicked the ball high in the air, and we practiced heading it. Everything was going fine until this one kid who I thought would probably be the starting goalie really blasted one in my direction. I could tell that if I stood where I was, the ball would go sailing over my head, so I started to backpedal in order to be in proper position, not realizing that the other line was not that far behind us. The first and last thing I heard was Paul yelling, "Look out! Let him get it!" and then my head crashed into something hard. The next thing I knew, I was lying on the ground with Chuck on top of me and the ball beside both of us.

Paul rushed over and started to pick me up. "Are you all right?"

"Just let me stay here a second," I whispered, jerking my hand free. In the meantime Chuck had rolled off of me and was trying to sneak away when he caught my eye. "Are you blind?" I yelled, still trying to catch my breath. "You're not even in our line, and besides, that was my ball!"

"I'm sorry, Richie," Chuck yelled back in an apologetic tone. "Paul told me to take it."

As I got up I looked over at Paul for an explanation. "No!" said Paul emphatically. "I meant for Chuck to look out and let you get the ball."

I turned around to continue yelling at Chuck, but now he was kneeling doubled over on the ground, rubbing his forehead in obvious pain. Seeing that made my anger disappear for a second, and when it returned all I had the heart to do was kick the ground and go back to my line.

A minute later I looked down at my shirt and noticed it was spotted with blood. Now I really felt awful, so I walked over to Chuck, pretending to ask again how he was, when I really was checking him over to see where he was bleeding from. I found nothing. Now my head was beginning to hurt a little more, and when I wiped my forehead I noticed fresh blood on my sleeve.

"I think I'm bleeding," I said softly to myself, and proceeded to walk off the field and go directly to the trainer. He took one look at my head and exclaimed, "Richie, you have a big gash in your forehead. I think we'd better get you to the hospital."

"Hospital? What for?"

"I don't want to take any chances with this," he said. "You may need stitches, and I want a doctor to look at it." The trainer couldn't stop the bleeding, so he wrapped a towel around my head and secured it in place with a belt.

Paul and Tony saw me walking off the field and they ran over to see what was happening.

"Where are you going?" asked Tony.

"They want me to go to the hospital to have my forehead looked at by the doctor. The trainer thinks I may need stitches."

"He doesn't know," said Paul. "It's probably just a small cut."

"I hope you're right," I yelled as I got into the trainer's car.

When I walked into the emergency room I really felt embarrassed with this towel on my head and all, so I was sort of glad when they put me in one of the rooms and closed the door. A nurse came in and removed the towel and cleaned my forehead with yellow stuff that burned. Then a doctor came in and examined me.

"You got a bad bite there, son."

"Bite?"

"Yeah, there's a set of teeth marks in your forehead."

"Teeth marks? How did I get teeth . . . That clumsy nerd."

"How did it happen?" asked the doctor.

"That Chuck, I'm going to kill him," I said.

"Chuck?" said the doctor.

"Yeah. This kid Chuck and I were playing soccer and we both went up to head the ball and . . . That turkey. Just when I thought he was coming around."

"You're going to need some stitches, son."

"Stitches?" I said. "No way. You're not putting any stitches in my head."

"I couldn't do it without your parents' permission anyway. Why don't you call home and let me talk to your parents?"

I reluctantly dialed my house and my mother answered. "Hi, Mom, it's me, Richie."

"How come you're calling? Did you miss the sports bus?"

"No, Mom, I had a little accident at practice." I heard my mother gasp. "It's nothing serious." I went on. "I just got a gash on my forehead and the doctor wants to put stitches in."

"Where are you now?" she asked.

"I'm in the emergency room at Mercy General Hospi-

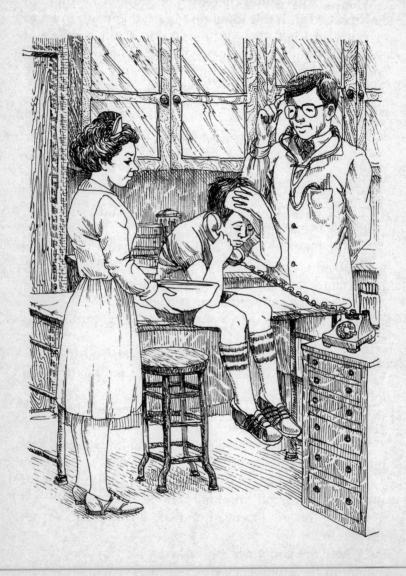

tal. Wait a second, the doctor wants to speak to you." I handed the phone to the doctor and sat down in a chair in the corner. I heard him say "Not serious" and then "Maybe fourteen stitches"—which didn't seem to go together—and then he hung up. "Your mom will be right over," he said as he left the room. *Fourteen stitches,* I thought. *There's no way my mother will let this doctor put fourteen stitches in my head.*

The phone was ringing just as we got home from the hospital. It was Paul. "Guess how many stitches I got."

"Ten," said Paul.

"Higher."

"Fifteen?"

"Lower."

"Fourteen?"

"Right. And guess how I got such a deep cut."

"What is this, twenty questions? How should I know?"

"Chuck bit me on the forehead."

"He what?"

"He bit me, and don't tell anybody, not even Tony. Okay?"

"Why don't you want me to tell Tony?" asked Paul.

"It's sort of embarrassing for people to know you've been bitten on the forehead." Almost before I'd finished, Paul began to laugh. "See what I mean?" I said.

"I wasn't laughing at that," said Paul, trying to pull himself together. "I was just thinking of something funny." I still wasn't amused by Paul's laughter, but I waited for him to finish. "I was just wondering if you could call a vampire who bites someone on the forehead instead of the neck a turkey vampire."

When I thought about it, that was sort of funny, but I wasn't much in the mood for humor right now. "Listen,

Paul," I said when he'd finally stopped laughing. "Don't forget your promise. Nobody is to know what happened."

"I won't tell anybody" was the last thing Paul said. But he did.

7

I was coming down the hall when Tony yelled at me, "Get bitten by a turkey vampire lately?" I pretended I didn't hear it the first time, but when he yelled it again, louder, I turned around and walked slowly toward him and Paul. This was my slow, angry gait. It's slow because it gives you time to think about what you're going to do. I had told Paul specifically not to tell anyone and he had promised he wouldn't. I could feel my face tightening up and the edges of my teeth rubbing together. If this were in my house and my brother or sister had seen me coming like this, there would be no mistaking how I was feeling and what was in store for them. I didn't think Tony or Paul knew what was coming.

I stood in silence for a second as the two of them continued to laugh at me. "Thanks a lot, Paul," I said.

Paul always wrinkles up his forehead when he pretends not to know what you are talking about. "What's the matter with you?" he asked.

I wasn't going to let him off the hook this time. He

knew darn well what he'd done. "You're a real jerk," I snapped.

Paul turned to Tony as if *he* had the answer to what he had done, and then he turned back to me. The perplexed look was still on his face.

"Forget it," I said, and I started to walk away from them.

I could hear someone running after me, yelling "Wait!" and then Paul grabbed my shoulder. "Will you wait a second?" pleaded Paul. "What's eating you, anyway?"

I looked down the hall at Tony, who was still standing in the same place, and then I looked straight at Paul. "You should know," I said, and turned slightly to give Paul the impression I was going to walk away again.

"Wait a second," said Paul, tightening his grip on my shoulder. "Honest! What did I do?"

"I thought you promised—" and when I said the word *promised,* Paul brought the palm of his hand up to meet his bowed forehead and blurted out, "I forgot, Richie. I'm sorry."

"Never mind." I jerked my shoulder away from him, and this time I did start to walk away.

"It was an honest mistake," said Paul, quickening his pace to catch up to me. "I'm sorry. What else do you want me to say?"

I didn't answer him.

"Since when are you Mr. Perfect?" yelled Paul. "Didn't you ever make a mistake?"

I don't know if Paul said anything else, but if he did I couldn't hear it because of the noise in the lunchroom. I got my lunch and purposely sat by myself at a different table than usual. It certainly wasn't fun eating lunch alone, but it was much better than eating with jerks. Out of the corner of my eye I thought I saw Tony and Paul looking over at me, but I never turned my head to see for sure.

"Hey, Richie."

I looked up. It was Chuck. I thought when I'd ignored him at the bus stop this morning that he would have gotten the hint that I was still annoyed at him.

"Are you okay, Richie?" he asked with an apologetic look on his face.

I stood up and raised my finger as if I were going to scold him, but instead I pointed it toward my forehead and said, "Do you see *Spalding* written up here?" Chuck looked puzzled; he shook his head no. "Well, then, here's a reminder for next time . . . *You're supposed to head the ball, not bite the head.*" And with that I got up and started to walk away.

To my surprise Chuck followed after, and when he caught up to me, he grabbed my arm and asked, "Wanna meet those girls today?"

I jerked my arm away and said, "Nope," in an abrupt fashion, hoping that he would leave.

"I told them all about you," he continued.

"Nope!"

"What great jokes you tell."

"Nope!" But this time it was a little less emphatic.

"How great you are in sports."

I could feel my annoyance fading. Maybe it wouldn't be such a bad idea after all. I stood up straight, brushed back the front of my hair with my hand, and was just about to say, "Wellll, all right," when I heard Chuck say, "How I bit you yesterday during the . . ." I couldn't believe he'd told them that. Now the whole school would know. How could I ever show my face in this building again?

My expression changed from one of delight to one of

murder. "I don't want to see anyone today," I snapped. My answer must have startled Chuck, because he took a step backward, and as he did, he bumped into a girl who was returning her dirty dishes to the window. Her tray went flying out of her hand and the dishes shattered into a million pieces when they hit the floor. Everyone in the lunchroom looked in my direction and cheered. Chuck helped the girl clean up the mess, and by the time he got up to say he was sorry to me, which he does all the time, I was gone.

At dinner my mother asked, "Do you feel all right?"

"I'm fine. Why?"

"You're not eating very much tonight. Do you feel sick?"

"Honest, Mom, I'm fine. I had a sandwich when I came home from soccer practice. It just killed my appetite. Listen, I have a lot of homework to do." I took my plate off the table and put it in the sink. "I'm going upstairs."

When I got to my room I turned on my radio and started to do my math. I tried to do the first problem four different ways, but nothing seemed to work out. I had no better luck on the second one either. I pushed my book aside, leaned back in my chair, and closed my eyes. As I started to drift off, I pictured myself with a broomstick in my hand and Paul with a pink rubber ball in his. Let's see, the last time we'd played stickball had been three years before, when we were eleven. Whenever Paul was losing, he'd start to cheat. Well, not exactly cheat, but he'd say a ball was fair when it was clearly foul or say he only had one out when he really had two. During this one game it was the last of the ninth with runners on second and third. There were two outs and the count was full. My next pitch was belt high and Paul swung at it and missed—but when I called him out he insisted that he checked his swing.

"You went around. I saw you," I insisted.

"I never broke my wrists," he replied.

"You did. I saw you!"

"I should know if I broke my wrists or not!"

"You're just a sore loser," I said.

"Well, if you don't like it, I'm going home," yelled Paul, throwing down the bat.

"Go home," I yelled back. "See if I care."

"Richie?"

"Huh?"

I looked up. I had been so involved in my thoughts that I hadn't heard my father come into the room. "You okay?" I didn't say a word. "Wanna talk?" I shook my head no. "I'll be in the den if you change your mind." He patted me a couple times on the shoulder and then disappeared downstairs.

I thought again about the stickball game. I couldn't remember who had called whom to apologize, but someone did, and by the next day everything was forgotten. I looked at my math assignment again and tried the first problem. *This whole thing is really dumb,* I thought. *If Paul is too stubborn to admit he was wrong, I'll just have to take the first step. I'll tell him I was having a bad day and then he'll tell me it was partly his fault and then everything will be okay. It still bugs me a little that I have to be the one to call him but . . . no buts, I'll just do it.* I closed my book. On the way into my mother's room the phone rang. It was Paul.

8

I hate to admit this: Tony was the ingredient that had been missing from our soccer team in previous years. But with him playing center forward and Paul and me playing wings, our team won our first four games easily. Today's game promised to be the hardest, however, and everyone knew that the winner of this one would probably be JV league champs for this year.

"Aren't you eating lunch today?" asked Paul.

"Naw, I'm not really hungry," I replied.

"You should eat something," said Paul. "It's not good to play on an empty stomach."

"What are you, my mother's representative here at school?" I snapped.

"Touchy, touchy," said Tony.

"Look, this is between Paul and me, so stay out of it."

Tony dropped his fork and arched his back slightly, as if he were a little shocked and angry at my reply. If anything, I should have been the one who was upset.

After all, he was the one who'd stuck *his* nose into *my* business.

"Look, you guys, forget it," said Paul, trying to smooth things over. "I think we're all a little uptight about today's game."

Tony relaxed in his seat.

"Maybe I will get a couple of pretzels and some chocolate milk after all," I said.

Paul opened his mouth as if he were going to say something, but he muttered "Forget it" under his breath and returned to eating his sandwich.

When I got to the locker room after school, Paul and Tony seemed to be talking about something they didn't want me to hear, because when they saw me they looked funny at each other and then got quiet.

"What's up?" I said.

"Nothing much," said Paul, continuing to look funny at Tony.

"What were you two just talking about?"

"Nothing," said Paul.

"English," said Tony.

"Whose father's driving which way on Friday?" said Paul, changing the subject.

"Friday? What's Friday?" I asked.

"The Get Acquainted Dance is on Friday," said Tony. "I think my father can take us there if one of your fathers can pick us up."

"I'll ask my father tonight," I said, "and I'll let you guys know tomorrow."

"Let's go out and kick the ball around," said Tony.

"See you outside soon," said Paul.

I started to ask them to wait up for me, but the two of them had already started to leave, so I said nothing. If I had really rushed I could have finished dressing in less than five minutes, but now there was no reason to, so I took my time.

When I arrived on the field, the team had just lined up to do its warm-up exercises. Coach Johnson then called us over to review the game plan and the starting lineup. "Good luck in today's game, boys. These guys are supposed to be the best. We are the best. Let's bow our heads for a little prayer before we go on the field." Everyone stood perfectly still in silence. "Go out there and give them hell," yelled Coach Johnson, and with a roar we took the field.

I don't know about Tony, but none of the rest of us had ever been on a soccer team that had a winning season. In the beginning of the first half we were extremely tight and disorganized, and before we knew it we were down 2–0. At that point the other team seemed to relax, and that's when we began to make our move. Tony stole the ball from their left fullback and with some very fancy footwork managed to get around him and score with a high shot into the right corner. Less than a minute later Paul headed one in on a corner kick, and just before the end of the half Tony scored again.

Tony took up where he'd left off at the end of the half and scored again, stealing the ball from the same fullback. I don't think the kid liked being embarrassed like that two times in the same game, and he raised his fist and said something I couldn't quite hear to Tony as he ran by to set up for the kickoff. This kind of verbal challenge happened so often that neither Tony nor anyone else on the team paid much attention to it.

We should have, because the next time down the field the fullback went for Tony instead of the ball, pushing him forward from behind. Tony was taken by surprise and tried to brace his fall by putting his arms out in front

of him. As he hit the ground I could swear I heard a crack, and then I saw him writhing in pain. Others said they'd heard a crack too.

Paul immediately ran over to Tony, with me trailing not far behind to offer help while play continued. "Are you all right?" Paul asked with concern.

"I don't know," said Tony, clutching his right wrist. "This hurts like hell!"

Coach Johnson and the ref knelt on the grass and gently inspected Tony's wrist. "Somebody get some ice," the coach yelled.

"I'll get some," I said. I ran to the sideline to look for the trainer.

By the time I returned a crowd had formed around Tony, and I had to fight my way into the center. I gave the ice to Tony, and he placed it gently on his wrist. "How does it feel now?" I asked. Tony had an awful look on his face, and all he could do was shake his head. Suddenly, without any warning, Paul began pushing his way furiously out through the crowd, knocking aside everybody he came in contact with, and took off in the direction of the visiting team's bench. About thirty feet from his destination he stopped, but only for a second, and then he resumed full speed toward the kid who had hurt Tony. The kid didn't realize until the last minute what Paul's intentions were, and by the time he did, he ended up tripping over his own feet as he started to back away. Paul took quick advantage of the situation, jumping on top of the fallen kid and pounding him in the head and chest. His advantage didn't last very long, however, because the kid was much bigger and stronger, and soon their positions were reversed. Paul was unable to break free, and he probably would have gotten pretty badly hurt if I hadn't arrived to pull the two of them apart.

Now the crowd of kids that had been around Tony had shifted their interest to us. "Lucky for you your friend saved you," taunted the kid as he wrestled to get free from his teammates' restraints.

"Come over here and say that," yelled Paul. "I should have broken your head open!"

"I should have broken your head open, too, but fortunately for you, you don't have one," he yelled back.

"Come try it, you jerk," yelled Paul.

That was probably a very dumb thing for Paul to say, because the other kid broke free and landed another blow to the side of Paul's face before I could release him. Paul went limp for a second and probably would have fallen to the ground if I hadn't supported his weight. He was silent for a moment, and then his body stiffened as he turned toward me. "Why didn't you let me go?" he asked angrily.

"I was trying to help you."

"By letting the guy hit me?"

"Is it my fault that he got away from . . ." But Paul walked away toward the sideline in search of Tony.

"Wait a second," I yelled. Paul continued to walk. "That's the thanks I get for trying to protect you. Next time you're on your own. You're a jerk! You know? A first-class jerk."

The ambulance was just arriving to take Tony to the hospital, so I walked over to watch, making sure to keep clear of Paul. As they loaded him on the stretcher and put him into the back of the van, he looked like he was in a lot of pain. Paul said something to him, pointing in my direction, and then returned to the game. I wanted to say something, too, like "Don't worry, everything will be okay," or "I don't know what Paul told you but whatever it was, it's not true." But the only thought that came to mind was *If it weren't for you, Paul wouldn't be acting like such a jerk.*

Sometimes I wonder where such awful thoughts come from. I don't think I really want to know.

Later that night Paul called me and told me that Tony had broken his arm in two places and that his arm would be in a cast for eight weeks. He didn't mention the fight, so neither did I. "Well, there goes our high-scoring trio," said Paul.

"Yeah, it's like old times now," I said. "Just you and me. Boy, this math test is going to be tough tomorrow. Do you believe that old man Martin gave us two whole chapters to—"

"Richie, didn't you hear what I said? Tony broke his arm in two places and he'll be out for the rest of the soccer season. Do you know what that will do to our team?"

"What do you think I am, deaf?" I sat up on the edge of the bed to emphasize what I was going to say next. "I heard what you said the first time. I think we can still win games without Tony. I score goals, too, you know. For that matter, so do you."

"You don't seem to care that Tony broke his arm," said Paul, clearly somewhat annoyed.

"How can you say I don't care?" I snapped back. "Didn't I get him ice for his arm?"

"Maybe it's just my imagination," said Paul, "but you've been acting sort of strange ever since you came home from camp. Every other day you're snapping out at me or Tony and—"

"That's not true," I interrupted, "so you and your imagination can drop dead!" I was so angry, I slammed down the phone and went into my room to study. I hadn't even gotten a chance to open my book when I heard the phone ring, and before my mother called me I knew it was Paul. For a·split second I debated whether to answer the phone or not.

He thinks he can insult me and then call back a few minutes later and say he's sorry. Well, he can't.

"Richie, Paul's waiting."

I purposely walked into my parents' room slowly.

"Richie, are you *going*—"

"I got it," I replied. "Hello," I said, still with an angry sound to my voice. "What do you want now?"

"I'm sorry I said what I said about you acting strange. I guess I was just upset about Tony breaking his arm and us losing the game."

I hesitated for just a moment and then said, "Don't lose any sleep over it. I already forgot about it."

"I won't take any more time," said Paul. "We both have a test to study for."

As I hung up the phone I should have felt a little sense of triumph. After all, I had won the argument with Paul and made him back down. But instead I had the same feeling I would have had if I had actually lost. Maybe I had lost, because deep down inside a voice was telling me Paul had been right when he'd said that I really didn't care about Tony's having been hurt. And to make matters worse, that same voice was saying that maybe I was even glad it had happened.

9

The Get Acquainted Dance was three days after Tony broke his wrist, and at lunch that day he told Paul and me that he was still in too much pain to go and have a good time.

"Look, if it will make you feel better," said Paul, "Richie and I will come over your house tonight and not go to the dance. Won't we, Richie?"

"Sure, there'll be other dances," I replied halfheartedly.

"No, you guys go and have a good time. I'll be all right."

That night while I was showering, I wondered what I really would have done if Tony had said, "Come over."

I don't know why I picked that night to shave for the first time, but I did. Whenever I had seen my father do it before, it had looked so easy. All you had to was wash your face with soap and then put on plenty of shaving cream and . . . The sides of my lips were so easy, but the middle . . . *How in the world do you get that indentation? Oh, I see, you just turn your hand this way and . . . oh, my*

God, I think I just cut out the middle third of my upper lip. No, that can't be, because if that were gone, there would be nothing to hold the sides of my lip on my face. If I lose any more blood, I'm going to need a transfusion. I'll just put this piece of toilet paper on the cut like this and press hard and ... I think it finally stopped. I'll keep the paper on my face until I get completely dressed. There, now. I looked at myself in the mirror to admire the finished product. Hair combed, clean shaven, a bandage on my forehead covering my vampire bite and a piece of paper hanging from my upper lip.

"Paul's here," my mother yelled up.

"Be right down," I said, and combed my hair one more time. "You're so gorgeous," I whispered under my breath, taking one final look. I raced down the stairs and grabbed my jacket. "Tell Dad not to come before eleven."

"Have a nice time, boys," my mom called. I'd already disappeared out the door.

When I got into the car, Paul had a strange look on his face. "Is something the matter?" I asked.

"What's that paper hanging from your lip?"

"Oh, that. I was shaving tonight for the first time and I cut my upper lip." I slowly peeled off the paper and showed the cut to Paul. "Is it very noticeable?"

"I don't think most people will notice that the middle part of your upper lip is missing the first time they look at you. I would never have thought twice about it if you hadn't pointed it out."

"No, really. How bad does it look?"

"You can hardly see it. Don't worry about it."

"Who's worried? I just asked a simple question."

"Forget it," said Paul.

"Gonna dance with the blonde tonight?"

"Are you kidding? I've been setting up my meeting

with her very carefully. Right now I almost have her eating out of my hand."

"But you haven't even talked to her yet."

"Don't sweat the small things. Just wait till we get to the dance and watch me operate."

This ought to be interesting, I thought. *He knows as much about operating on girls as I know about operating on brains.*

The dance was already pretty crowded by the time we arrived. There were very few people dancing. However, most of the boys were against one wall, while the girls were against the other.

"The girls just can't keep their eyes off me," said Paul as we picked out our spot on the wall.

"It's obvious why," I said with a straight face, knowing that Paul would certainly pick up the bait.

"Tell me why."

"All the girls are staring at you because your fly is open."

"Oh, my God." He turned to check it.

"Gotcha," I said with a laugh.

"You jerk."

"Hey, Paul, look at that girl over there."

"Where?" said Paul. "There are only fifty girls standing over there."

"There, next to the window," I told him, motioning with my head.

"The tall girl in the blue skirt?"

"No, next to her."

"The short, fat redhead?"

"She's not fat," I said.

"She ain't thin."

"Okay. Then who do you think is so terrific?"

Paul looked around for a minute and then pointed to a tall girl in a short skirt who was dancing. "That one."

"Too skinny."

"Too skinny? Your taste stinks," said Paul.

"What about Pimple Patty, the girl you took to the graduation dance last year?"

"That was a different story," said Paul.

"Tell me about it," I said. "Hey, isn't that the blonde?"

"Where?" asked Paul.

"Are you blind? There!"

"That's not her," replied Paul.

"It sure is," I insisted.

"You're mistaken. But even if it is, now isn't the time to make my move. Now is the time to cruise a little. Look over there. That girl really looks like action."

"Well, what are you waiting for?" I asked. "Move on in."

"There's plenty of time left for that. I want to check out all the other girls first," said Paul.

"*Chicken*," I said. "You probably wouldn't know what to do anyway."

"And who's going to teach me, you?"

"Sure, when do you want the professor to start?"

"Hey, look," said Paul, "aren't those the girls we see sitting with Chuck at lunch?" Sure enough, there by the refreshment stand were Jill and Ellen. "Let's walk around to the other side of the gym."

"No, you walk if you want. I'm going to stay right here for a while."

"Suit yourself," said Paul. "If we don't meet up before, look for me about ten-thirty."

When I was sure Paul was far enough away, I started to move in the opposite direction, over to the refreshment stand. By the time I got there Jill had already gotten her soda, but Ellen was still in line, so I sort of pushed my way up behind her and tried to muster up enough courage to introduce myself. *How do you start?* I thought. *How about, "Can I buy you a soda?" Not bad, but sodas are free. No sense beating around the bush. I'll just say, "Hi, my name is Richie. Would you like to dance?" And she'll say, "I'd love to." See how easy it is. There's one catch. I can't dance. How about if I just introduce myself and see what happens?* I cleared my throat, picked up my head, and blurted out, "Hi, my name is Richie." Unfortunately, Ellen had gotten her soda while I was looking at the floor, so instead of talking to her, I was staring face to face with the guy giving out the sodas.

"Hi, my name is Brad. Do you want Coke or Seven-Up?"

I turned to look for Ellen. She was nowhere to be found.

"Coke or Seven-Up?" asked Brad again.

"Ehh, nothing," I said. Brad looked at me with that boy-are-you-weird look as I turned and left.

"I thought you were going to stay over there," Paul remarked.

I wondered if my face was still red. "I just went to the bathroom. Did you talk to the blonde yet?"

"I was on my way over to get a soda—"

"And when you finish that," I interrupted, "you're going to go over and ask her to dance!"

"How did you know that?" said Paul with some surprise in his voice.

"I guess I'm a mind reader," I answered. When Paul left to get a soda, I scanned the gym to see if I could locate Ellen again. She was nowhere to be found. I'd started to walk over to the other side of the gym to check out one last spot when I felt someone grab my arm. At first I thought it was Paul, but when I looked it turned out to be a girl I had never seen before.

"Wanna dance?" she asked.

She had big green eyes and an infectious smile and a look on her face that said she wasn't taking no for an answer. "I don't dance very well," I said.

"That's okay. Just watch me and I'll show you how." The girl began to move her left leg and right arm, and then her right leg and left arm, alternately, in time to the music. "See, it's easy. First the left and then the right. Now you try it."

I started with my left leg and my left arm, and when I tried to switch to the other arm, my leg switched too. I really felt very foolish, but the girl didn't seem to mind as she continued to dance around me. When the music stopped, I headed off the floor, but the girl ran after me and grabbed my arm again. "Hey, I don't even know your name."

"Richie," I said, continuing to move away.

"Hi, Richie, my name's Gina. Where are you running to?"

"I have to find my friend Paul. I promised I'd meet him over by the refreshments."

"I'll walk you over," said Gina. "I'd like a soda too."

I didn't bother to answer because it didn't seem to make any difference anyway. When I got to the refreshment stand I got a Coke for Gina and myself and pretended to look for Paul. I was really still looking for Ellen.

"What does your friend look like? Maybe I can help you look for him," said Gina.

"He's too difficult to describe. I can find him okay by myself."

"Great dance, isn't it?"

"Yeah," I replied while continuing to look around. "Hey,

look," I blurted, "I've got to go now." I had spotted Ellen in the far corner and now bolted off in that direction. This time I kept my eye on her, but it wouldn't have mattered, since she was very much involved in a conversation with another girl. When she finally noticed I was standing behind her, she turned and gave me a warm, friendly smile. I smiled back and then blurted out, "HimynameisRichie."

"I know that," she replied.

"You do?"

"You're in my biology class, aren't you?"

"Oh, yeah," I replied, feeling sort of stupid. "How about if I start things all over again?" I took two steps backward and then approached her again. "Anything exciting happen to you today since biology?" Ellen started to chuckle.

"How's your sister doing?"

"How do you know I have a sister?"

"It was a lucky guess. You just look like you have one. Maybe even a twin."

"Who told you?"

I was about to say *I read your mind* when someone tapped me on the shoulder.

"How about another dance?" asked Gina.

"What?" I replied with some embarrassment.

"Dance? Want to dance?"

I looked at Ellen, hoping she would say something to get me out of this, but she didn't, and for some reason I couldn't say no. "I'll look for you afterward," I said as Gina led me to the floor. This time the music was slower, so it was easier to follow Gina and keep my eye on Ellen. An awkward silence followed. I knew it was up to me to say something, but for one of the few times in my life nothing came to mind.

"Do you like sports?" asked Gina.

Sports, I thought. *I could talk all day about sports. Do you want to talk about baseball or football or maybe basketball?* "Yeah," I replied. My lips and tongue seemed paralyzed.

"Do you play any?"

"I play soccer and I'm also going to try out for basketball and I like to watch football on TV and I might go out for track." I had to pause to take a breath. "You know, the soccer team is seven and one. We lost our last game but only because the other team played dirty. They purposely hurt Tony. He's one of our star players. The reffing was awful."

I probably would have continued talking, but a funny thing happened. For no apparent reason Gina seemed to move closer to me. At first I thought it felt good, but then the gym began to feel extremely hot and my collar felt like a vise that was closing. The more I tried to back away, the more it seemed that Gina tightened her grip. I think three of my ribs would have been crushed if the record hadn't ended.

"Listen, Gina, I think my friend might be looking for me outside!" And with that I broke free and walked back to the corner where I'd left Ellen. She was gone, and to make matters worse, Gina was hot on my trail. When I saw her heading in my direction, all I could think of was to get away from her, and instinctively I ran to the first door I could find and pushed it open. I was surprised to find myself outside, but the cold air felt good on my face and it was a relief to be away from—

"It feels so nice out here." Gina's voice was unmistakable.

For a second I was dumb enough to think she hadn't seen me yet, so I ducked down and started to walk slowly around to the front of the building.

"Wait for me," she yelled. This time I broke into a trot. I looked over my shoulder to see where she was now, but the light was so poor I really couldn't tell. Just before I reached the far corner of the building I thought I heard a noise behind me, and I quickened my pace. As I turned the corner a tree or a bush or something sprang up in front of me and before I could put the brakes on I crashed into it. The next thing I knew I was flat on my back in a pile of leaves, staring into the face of Coach Johnson.

"Richie, are you all right?"

I stood up and pulled some wet leaves out of the collar of my shirt as I tried to catch my breath.

"Are you okay?" asked Coach Johnson again.

I cleared my throat and was just about to say, "It was so hot in there I came out to get some fresh air," but all I had a chance to say was "It was so hot—" before I was interrupted, first by Gina's voice yelling, "Richie, is that you, Richie?" and then by her in person. Coach Johnson took one look at me and one look at Gina and then he dropped his head, I think to cover a smile.

"I think the two of you better go inside," he said.

"It's not what you think," I said as he followed us to the entrance of the gym. "I was really just getting some fresh air." Coach Johnson looked at the two of us one more time and smiled as he left us standing side by side near the door.

"When is your next soccer game? I'd like to come watch you play."

I had never met a girl quite like Gina before—not that I had met many girls before—and I wasn't sure right now if I liked her persistence or not. *If I answer her,* I thought, *then she'll ask me another question. However, if I don't answer*

her, she'll probably ask me another question anyway. I started to say, "My next game is on Tuesday ..." but I never got *Tuesday* out because I had spotted Paul across the other side of the gym, talking to Ellen.

"Your next game is when?" asked Gina again.

"Excuse me," I said as I rather abruptly walked away from her and over to where Paul was.

10

"There you are," said Paul at my approach. "I couldn't find you, so I came over here to talk to—"

I grabbed Paul by the arm and pulled him toward me. "Having fun?"

"All I was doing was asking her where—"

"I thought we had a pact."

"We do," insisted Paul.

"Didn't I see this girl first?"

"Of course you did. No one said you didn't. Now, will you shut up for a second and let me explain?"

"This better be good," I snapped, squeezing his arm a little harder.

"Let go of my arm, you're hurting me," said Paul. He'd raised his voice just enough for the people around us to turn around and begin to take notice.

"Oh, you found your best friend," said Gina, who had followed me over.

I can't say that I'm proud of the things that happened next.

"You're lucky that's all I hurt!" I said, and let his arm drop. "The other night on the phone you said that I was the one who was acting strange. Try looking in the mirror if you want to see a strange one."

"I don't know what you're so upset about. I was just waiting here for you and talking to Ellen."

"Upset! You don't know why I'm so upset. Tell me how you would feel if your supposed best friend decided he didn't like you anymore—"

"Now, wait a second. That's not—"

"No, you wait . . . and he started spending more time with someone else." I saw Paul grit his teeth and shake his head from side to side in disagreement, but I continued. "Then you made Chuck bite me, and in our last game when I came to help you, you blamed me when the other kid hit you. I was willing to overlook all of this, but when I saw you horning in on Ellen, that was the last straw. As far as I'm concerned, we're through. After my father drops you off tonight don't bother to call me anymore. Understand?"

"Yeah, I understand," said Paul. "Forget about giving me a ride home. I think I'd rather go home with someone else."

"That's fine with me. Good-bye!" Ellen and Gina had been silent throughout all of this, and I wanted to apologize to them before I left. I looked first at Ellen, then at Gina, and I could tell by their expressions that both thought I had acted like a jerk and I could kiss my chances with both of them good-bye. Somehow, saying "I'm sorry" didn't seem to mean much here, so I turned and walked outside to wait for my father.

"Where's Paul?" asked my father as I got into the car. When I didn't answer, he started to repeat his question, but stopped when he saw my face. I'm not sure he could tell that I was almost ready to cry, but he asked, "What happened?" I still wouldn't answer. I guess he got a little mad then, because he said, "I'm not going anywhere until you tell me where Paul is."

I looked back at my father, who was staring right back at me. I knew he meant business.

"We had a fight, okay? Not a fight fight but a fight. He's getting a ride with someone else. Satisfied? Now will you take me home?"

My father looked at me for a second, and then he started the car. We spent the ride home in complete silence.

11

The next morning I was up at about six and unable to fall back to sleep. I tried to push the incident at the dance out of my mind, but unfortunately everything I tried thinking about eventually led back to Paul. I dressed quietly and went outside to shoot baskets. It was a beautiful morning, the kind of morning that Paul and I used to . . . Damn, see what I mean? And to make matters worse, I couldn't get any of my shots to drop. After fifteen minutes of this I gave up and put the ball back in the garage. Saturday morning is probably the worst time to watch TV, with all those stupid cartoons, so I decided to take a walk. Halfway down the block I thought I heard someone softly calling my name. I stopped for a second to listen, and when I heard nothing, I continued walking.

"Richie!"

This time it was a little louder, but the voice was still too far away to be recognized. I turned around and there, halfway down the block, was Chuck. As he approached, I could see he was wearing jeans, an old college sweatshirt, and sneakers that looked like they'd just been put on for the first time. When he got to where I was, I had the urge to run the bottom of my sneaks over the tops of his to dirty them; but I didn't.

"I heard you and Paul were in a fight last night at the dance," he whispered as he approached.

"You don't have to whisper. No one can hear you. It wasn't a fight fight. Were you at the dance?"

"No, something came up and I couldn't go."

"How did you hear about it?"

"Ellen called me last night around eleven-thirty. She told me that you and Paul had been yelling at each other but she wasn't sure why."

I could feel myself getting angry all over again. "How would you feel if your supposed best friend tried to steal your girlfriend at a school dance. Huh?"

"I never got that far with a girl to have to worry about it, but if I did, I wouldn't like it one bit either."

"After last night Ellen probably thinks I'm a real jerk for the way I acted, and she wouldn't want to go out with me even if someone paid her to." I waited for a second to see if Chuck would say something to prove that wasn't true, but when he didn't, I asked, "Did she say anything to you about me?"

Chuck wrinkled up his forehead as if he were in deep thought and then, after a few seconds, said, "Nope."

"It doesn't matter anyway!"

"You know something, Richie? You were right. Paul is a real jerk. If I were you, I would have smashed him one right in the face." He flung an uppercut at an imaginary person in front of him.

"Thanks. Hey, what are you doing walking around so early on a Saturday, anyway?"

"I do this every Saturday. Usually no one is out at this time."

Then I got a great idea. *Since Chuck thinks I'm right and since he knows Ellen very well, maybe I could ask him to put in a good word for me. Maybe he could even take me over sometime when he goes over. But that would be using him. Well, it wouldn't be using him that much—after all, didn't he say he would introduce me to the girls before all of this happened?*

"My house is just down the block. Want to come over and shoot baskets?" The whole thing still didn't feel very good, but I did it anyway.

Chuck hesitated for a second before answering. "I'm not very good."

"That's okay," I replied. When we got to my driveway I said, "Let me get the ball." I wish I'd been able to use somebody other than Chuck, but I was desperate to make things right with Ellen, and he was the only one who could help me.

"Here," I said, flipping him the ball. Chuck caught it awkwardly with two hands. He walked up as close as he could to the tip of the rim without getting under it and with all his might pushed the ball wildly up into the air. As quickly as the ball went up, it came down, without hitting anything but air. Chuck looked back at me and said, "See, I told you."

I had to hold my teeth together and look away or else I would surely have laughed out loud. *You can say that again,* I thought, but said nothing. "Come over here and let me show you how to shoot a lay-up," I said as I retrieved the ball. Chuck walked over to where I was standing and waited for me to continue my instructions. "Come over here," I continued, moving to the right of the basket. Chuck followed without a word. "Now pick out an imaginary spot on the backboard and push the ball off your fingertips, like this, and try to hit the spot." Chuck watched intently as the ball hit the backboard and fell dead center into the basket. The ball came back to me on one bounce and I scooped it up. "Here, you try it."

Chuck put the ball into the palm of his hand and pushed it hard; it hit the backboard with too much force and bounced off the front lip of the basket.

"Just do it easy," I said, showing him again. "Pick out that spot and ..." The ball went in again. "Remember, easy."

Chuck retrieved the ball and went to the spot I'd marked for him to the right of the basket. He took a deep breath and a very serious look appeared on his face. He studied his task for a long time and finally pushed the ball off his fingertips again, only much easier this time. It went right in. "It's in!" he yelled, fist in the air.

"Again," I said. "You need to put in ten in a row before you can move on to the next step." I threw him the ball and found a comfortable spot on the grass behind the basket to watch.

"That's it ... soft touch ... off your fingertips ... pick out that spot ... great, I think you've got it."

Chuck put the basketball down beside me and lay down on the cool grass to catch his breath. The intense look he'd been wearing melted into a smile and a look of accomplishment.

"Boy, this is really terrific," said Chuck. "Nobody ever took the time to show me how to do this before. Having friends must be great."

"So you think having a friend is so great," I replied with some bitterness in my voice. "Look what happened with my so-called friend. Lately every time we got together all he would do was argue. And look how he messed up things now with me and Ellen."

"Why would Paul do that to you?"

"Ever since Tony moved in, Paul has been different. He spends so much time with Tony, it's as if I don't exist anymore. But that's okay. It's his loss, not mine."

"At least you have friends to lose," said Chuck with some sadness in his voice. "Hey, listen, I have to go. My parents will wonder where I am. I wish there were something I could do for you to repay you for today."

Well, here's my chance. No, I can't do it. "Forget it," I said.

Chuck got up and started down the driveway; but halfway down he turned to face me. There was a big smile on his face. "Listen, Richie," he said. "I had planned to visit Ellen this afternoon. How about if we go over together and I can introduce you to her."

That was his idea, now, not mine. I'd had nothing to do with it. *Say yes. What are you waiting for now? Remember, every time you get involved with Chuck something goes wrong. But what can go wrong here? I meet him, we walk over to Ellen's house, he introduces me to her, and that's all I need him for. There's no way he can mess this up.*

"Okay," I said hesitantly. "What time and where?"

"Two-thirty, in front of my house," he said as he started walking away.

"I'll be there," I yelled to him. *This will fix Paul good,* I thought. *And as far as Chuck goes, this is a straight one-for-one deal. I played ball with him and he's giving me an intro. All debts are canceled. I never promised to be his friend.* Besides, I wasn't in the market for any other friends right then.

12

"What are you all dressed up for?" asked my mother.

"Dressed up? I just put on some new jeans and a new shirt. Is that dressed up?"

"Are you going someplace?"

"Me? No. I mean, yes. Well, not exactly. I'm just going out for a walk. What time is dinner tonight?"

"Around five-thirty."

"I'll be home by five," I said, then scooted out the door to avoid any more questions. Chuck's house wasn't far away. When I got there, he was already waiting for me outside. Slung over his left shoulder was a large brown burlap bag.

"What's that?" I asked.

"Ellen and Jill like animals, so I brought along my snake," he replied without batting an eyelash.

My eyes widened, and if they hadn't been attached somewhere inside my head, I'm sure they would have fallen out. "You brought your what?" I asked.

"My snake Julius," he replied. "Julius is a baby boa. His full name is Julius Squeezer."

"Boa as in constrictor?" I asked.

Chuck put the bag on the ground, untied the drawstring, and pulled the edges apart. "Richie, meet Julius. Julius—Richie."

I leaned over from where I stood and looked into the top of the bag. Coiled up in a heap at the bottom was a green, red, and copper–colored boa constrictor. At first I couldn't find the head, but in a few seconds it slowly appeared from among the coils.

"I know they love animals."

What I really wanted to say next was *For God's sake, Chuck, take that snake home immediately,* but instead I said, "Gee, Chuck, he's great. Do you really think the girls will want to meet your snake?"

"It will be a great surprise," he said. He closed the bag and started walking.

I tried to collect my thoughts regarding what I was going to say to Ellen when I got there, but all I could think of was *Gimme a* B, *gimme an* O, *gimme an* A. *What do you get? Boa. Boa. Boa!!!*

"We're here."

"We're where?" I asked.

"That's the house over there," said Chuck, pointing to a half-stone, half-brick ranchhouse. I followed Chuck across the street and he rang the bell. A short, older woman opened the door and motioned for us to come in.

"Hi, Mrs. Phillips. This is my friend, Richie." I nodded my head as Chuck continued. "Where are the girls?"

"They're downstairs," said Mrs. Phillips with a smile. "Go ahead down. They're expecting you."

"Follow me, Richie," said Chuck. He preceded me

through the dining room and kitchen to a stairway leading down to a large paneled rec room.

"Hi," said Chuck enthusiastically as he bounced down the stairs. I followed cautiously behind him, taking one step at a time. Chuck put the bag down in the middle of the floor and ran over to hug the girls while I stood beside the bottom step and fiddled with some loose change in my pocket. Things were so dry inside my mouth that my tongue felt glued to the top and I found myself trying to peel it free, just in case I had to speak. Both girls looked over at me with expressions that made me feel like I was from outer space.

"Hi," said Ellen.

"Hi," I replied. I don't know if I should have said what I said next, but it just seemed to come out before I could stop it. "I want to explain about last night."

"Richie, this is Jill," interrupted Chuck.

"Hi, Jill," I replied, turning a little to the left to acknowledge her presence and then quickly back to Ellen to continue what I had started. "I'm really not what you think I am."

Before Ellen had a chance to reply, Jill pointed to the bag and asked, "What's in there?"

"I thought you'd never ask," said Chuck. He undid the drawstring, and before anyone had a chance to say anything else, he had turned the bag upside down, dumping the snake onto the rec room floor. I was glad I had chosen to stay by the stairs, because the snake started to slither toward the girls. Ellen and Jill gasped in unison and took a couple of steps backward.

"Girls, meet Julius."

"Is that thing real?" asked Jill.

"If it isn't, I'd like to know how he makes it move," said Ellen.

Chuck went over and picked Julius up at the thickest part of his body and waved him confidently in the air. "He's only a baby. See, he's harmless." Julius coiled the back part of his body around Chuck's upper arm, stiffening the front portion up at a forty-five-degree angle and raising his head almost eye level with Chuck. I don't think snakes can really smile, but it looked to me as if Julius had a broad smile on his face just before he opened his mouth and bared his teeth at Chuck. The color on Chuck's face changed first to pale green and then ghost-white as he walked almost in a dazed state over to a chair, where he deposited Julius. Julius immediately started to coil himself around the back of the chair with such intensity, you could hear the chair straining under the pressure. Chuck looked first at me and then at the girls before mechanically repeating, "He's never done that before. He's never done that before. He's never done that before."

Suddenly I had the sensation that everyone in the room was staring at me. *If they expect me to do anything with that snake, they're crazy. I'll just tell them that I'm allergic to boa constrictors. They make me break out all over. No, I'll be honest and tell them the truth. I'm too young to die. They can't argue with that. And besides, you predicted something like this was going to happen. You knew it. You came over to patch up things with Ellen and . . .*

"Richie," whined Chuck from the corner, "will you help me put Julius back in the bag?"

"Please help him," pleaded Jill and Ellen together.

"Sure, I'll help," I said with such confidence in my voice that I almost believed it myself for a split second. I cupped my hands around my mouth like a megaphone and shouted, "Okay, everybody, let's calm down! First of all, sudden movement makes a boa nervous, so if you have to move, do it slowly." I think I'd heard someone on

TV say that but, true or not, it sounded good. "Second, Jill, you go get the bag, and Ellen, you—"

"You want me to get the bag?" asked Jill.

"You want to help, don't you?"

"Do as he says," pleaded Chuck.

"Now, Ellen, start talking to Julius. Coax him off the chair and tell him to go into the bag."

"Why me?"

"Because boas are soothed by female voices and they're more likely to listen."

"Who told you that?"

I hadn't been prepared for so many questions, so I cleared my throat twice to give myself time to think up an answer. "The next time we're in the library I'll show you. It says so in the uh, uh, *New American Wild Animal Encyclopedia*." Ellen glanced over her shoulder at me in disbelief. "Honest, I'd show you if you had volume ten or eleven, I'm not sure which one, here."

Ellen inched close to the snake, and when she'd gotten about a foot from him, she began to talk to him in her sexiest voice. "Okay, Julie, baby, enough of this nonsense. Now, when I count to three, you jump off the chair right into the bag." Jill opened the top of the sack and pointed it at Julius. "*One . . . Two . . . Three . . .*" Julius cocked his head to one side as if he'd understood everything Ellen had said, and he responded with a loud hissing sound that startled everyone.

"I think he said no!" said Ellen.

"Now what'll we do, Richie?" asked Chuck.

"Listen, Chuck," I said. "I think I've got another good idea. How about if I circle around the chair this way, and when Julius follows me, you can circle around the chair the other way and throw the bag over his head?" I didn't wait for Chuck to answer. "Here, take the bag and wait for my signal."

I tiptoed around to the left and Julius followed my every movement. When his head was turned completely around, I cleared my throat and motioned with my eyes for Chuck to go around to the right. With the bag held high over his head Chuck moved closer to the unsuspecting snake. When Chuck was almost on top of him, I nodded my head again, signaling him to drop the bag. Julius must have sensed something, because just as Chuck was about to lower the bag the snake turned and lunged at him. Chuck jumped to the left to avoid the snake, and this brought him face to face with me when he brought the bag down.

I could see Chuck's half-apologetic, half-frightened face through the burlap covering, and I clenched both hands in strangling position and followed him as he backed slowly away from me. I don't think I would have really killed him or even hurt him, but whatever I would have done was interrupted by the laughter coming from behind me.

"Which way do you like him better? With or without the bag?" asked Ellen.

"It matches his pants perfectly," said Jill.

Somehow this whole incident didn't seem as funny to me as it did to everyone else, and I ripped off the bag and threw it in the direction of the chair. I guess the bag flying by the chair scared Julius, because the next thing I heard was Ellen and Jill yelling, "The snake, the snake . . . it's crawling into the bag. It's crawling into the bag!"

Sure enough, Julius had almost completely disengaged himself from the chair and was slithering along the floor toward the bag. When he reached the edges of the burlap, he parted them with his head and continued forward into the bag. Chuck ran over to the bag just as Julius's tail disappeared inside, and he pulled the drawstrings tight and tied them in three secure knots.

Raising the bag high in the air, he exclaimed, "Everyone can relax now. The danger is over." He then walked proudly over to the corner and deposited the bag before looking back at us and asking, "Well, what do we do now?"

"I just got a new album," Jill announced. "Who wants to come up to my room and hear it?"

"I do," said Chuck.

When I didn't respond right away, Jill looked over at me.

"Naw, you go ahead. I'm not in the mood for music right now."

"I'll stay here with Richie," said Ellen.

Jill and Chuck went upstairs and an uncomfortable silence followed.

"Are you going to stay mad the rest of the afternoon?" asked Ellen.

How did she expect me to answer that question?

"You did look rather funny with that bag over your head."

It wasn't very funny to me, I thought.

"Look at this," said Ellen, and with that she got a trash bag and began shouting, "Okay, Chuck, now you go this way and I'll go that way and you do this and I'll do that but if you do that then I'll do this and . . ."

The imitation was perfect, and I felt the corners of my lips curving upward despite my every effort to stop them.

"Not bad, a little smile. We're making progress."

"Wanna start over again?" I asked.

"Sure," said Ellen.

"Hi, my name is Richie." I was an old pro at this part

already. "Aren't you in Mrs. Singer's biology class? Turn around and let me see the back of your head." Ellen turned around. "Yes, I'd recognize the back of that head anywhere."

"And aren't you Richie Harmon, the famous soccer player and snake trainer?"

"The one and only!" I said with a deep bow.

"Now, what were you saying before we were so rudely interrupted? Something about your not being what you seem to be."

"Did I say that?"

"Yeah, you said you wanted to explain something about the dance last night."

"I did? Oh, yeah, I did, but I forgot what it was."

"That's okay. You don't have to explain."

"I don't?"

"Not really. But tell me the truth. Is there really an *American Wild Animal Encyclopedia*?"

I didn't bother to answer. Instead I just smiled. "Why don't you come and see me play soccer sometime? Our team's not that bad. We were in first place until Tony— that's one of the guys on the team—got hurt, and since then we've lost two games, so now we're in second place."

"What kind of a player is Chuck?"

"Are you kidding? He has a rough time walking and chewing gum at the same time."

"Why don't the guys like Chuck?"

Ellen certainly knew how to ask tough questions. "Because," I said with a smile, realizing how dumb that answer was.

"You want to elaborate?"

"Because he just doesn't fit in."

"Oh," said Ellen. She decided not to press the issue further. "What else do you like to do?"

I breathed a sigh of relief. "I like football and baseball and I guess all kinds of sports. How about you?"

"I'm not very good at sports, but I like to watch them. When is your next soccer game?"

"You mean you'll come and watch?"

"If you tell me when it is."

"Next Thursday is our last game. Three o'clock. After school. On the new soccer field. Three o'clock on Thursday."

"Want something to eat or drink?"

"What time is it?"

"Four-thirty."

"Four-thirty? You're kidding. I have to go home. We eat dinner early on Saturday."

Chuck and Jill were in the kitchen drinking soda when we walked upstairs.

"I gotta go now, Chuck."

"So do I, but first I have to go down and get Julius."

In the time it took Chuck and Jill to come back, I asked Ellen for her number, and she wrote it down for me on a piece of her flowered notepaper.

"I had a nice time today," said Ellen with a smile in her voice.

"Me too. Don't forget Thursday three o'clock."

"Three o'clock Thursday," repeated Ellen.

On the way home Chuck asked, "Do you like Ellen?"

"Sure, but don't tell her I said that. I heard it's better if girls worry a little."

"Okay. I won't," said Chuck as he disappeared into his house.

When I got home my mother was in the kitchen fixing dinner. "Is that you, Richie?"

"Yep," I replied.

"Where did you go?"

"Out."

"What did you do?"

"Nothin' "

"Did you have a good time?"

"Yup," I yelled, and disappeared upstairs. "Terrific," I whispered to myself.

13

By lunchtime Monday everyone in the school knew about the fight. I passed Paul a couple of times in the hall but didn't say a word to him, and he didn't seem to want to talk to me either. At lunch Paul got to our old table first, so I decided to sit with Ellen.

"Mind if I sit here?"

"Make yourself comfortable," said Ellen. "Chuck's sick today, so it will just be the three of us."

"The two of you," chimed in Jill. "I'm not very hungry today, so I thought I'd go over to the library and work on my history report. The rough copy is due Friday."

I wasn't sure if Jill had made up the story or not, but I certainly wasn't going to stop her. I waited for her to leave before I spoke. "I had fun yesterday."

"So did I," agreed Ellen.

"Do you have a bike?" Ellen nodded. "If you don't have anything planned for this weekend, I could ride my bike over and we could go out riding."

"I know a perfect place we can go that's not far from here."

I was just about to ask where, when I was interrupted by a familiar voice from behind. "I'd like to talk to you for a second."

"Where is the place you were talking about?" I asked.

Ellen didn't seem to know what to do as her eyes shifted from me to Paul and back.

"I'd like to talk to you for a second," repeated Paul.

You may want to talk to me but there's no way I'm ever talking to you, I thought. But I didn't say anything.

"I would really like to talk to you," said Paul, raising his voice a little. I continued to stare directly at Ellen without saying a word. Paul was so close to me, I could hear his every breath. I don't know how long we were there, but finally Paul stamped his foot on the floor in disgust as he said, "Damn you, Richie," and left.

Ellen looked at me as if she didn't know exactly what to say. To tell the truth, neither did I, so I picked up my bag of potato chips and offered it to her. She shook her head, so I put the bag back down. "What were you saying before?"

Ellen might still be staring at me if it weren't for a girl at the next table who asked, "Hey, Ellen, do you understand how to do the third math problem we have for homework?" Ellen reached under the table to get her math book, and she studied it for a second before she replied, "Sure. Come over here and I'll show you how to do it." As the girl changed chairs Ellen looked over at me and said, "Richie, meet Sally. Sally—Richie." We acknowledged each other briefly and Ellen immediately shifted her attention from me to Sally.

"First you draw the figure and put in all your . . ."

I wonder what Ellen thought of my not talking to Paul?

"Then you put down the formula for . . ."

If she knew the facts, I'm sure she'd agree with me.

"Now get all your x's on one side and the . . ."

She was at the dance. She knows exactly what he's like. I've got nothing to be ashamed of. Why does she keep looking over at me? I think I'd better go. "Listen, Ellen," I said as I stood up, "I just remembered something I forgot in my locker. I'll call you tonight." On my way out I walked past my old table, but I didn't look at Tony or Paul at all. Well, maybe I looked at them a little out of the corner of my eye, but I'm sure they never knew it.

That night, right after dinner, I called Ellen and we made plans to go riding on Saturday. I was sort of relieved to see that she wasn't angry with me for what had happened at lunch. Anyway, I'd known she wasn't angry all along. No sooner had I hung up from speaking with Ellen than Gina called. I don't remember exactly what we talked about, but it was okay hearing from her. I don't know why, but I seemed to have a lot of homework for a Monday night and before I knew it, it was ten-thirty. Before I went to sleep I looked again at the two A's and one B I had gotten back today from tests I had taken the week before. Everything was falling into place now. Two girls interested in me, good marks in school, basketball season just around the corner, a date with Ellen for Saturday, everything. I guess with all of that I should have been very happy. Shouldn't I? Well, I wasn't. And I knew until I settled things between Paul and me, I never would be.

14

When I made a special effort to avoid Paul completely on Tuesday, I realized that on this day alone our paths crossed twenty-seven times. I think I caught him looking back at me out of the corner of his eye, but I pretended not to notice. Once he was headed straight for me and probably would have knocked me down if I hadn't crossed over to the other side of the hall. By last period things had gotten pretty ridiculous, between his pretending not to look and my crossing over, and at one point I think I saw him cover up a smile as I walked by. *If this keeps up,* I thought, *it will take me at least twenty minutes to weave my way down the hall to class, and I'll probably be seasick when I get there.*

I don't think I'd been home from school five minutes when the phone rang. "Aren't you guys ever going to talk to each other again?" It was Tony. At first I was taken aback by his question, but then I got real mad.

"Did Paul put you up to this?"

"Are you crazy? If he knew I was calling you he'd have my head."

Then why are you calling me? I thought. *If I were in your shoes I'd be more than happy to have Paul all to myself and have you out of the way.* "Maybe I'll give him a break and say a few words to him someday," I said smugly.

"But you were such good friends!"

"Were," I echoed. "Now, are there any other brilliant things you want to say? I have a lot of homework to do."

"As a matter of fact, there are," said Tony, much to my surprise. "I don't understand why you're continuing to act like such a jerk when deep down I really don't think you are one. Good-bye!"

"Wait a second!" I blurted out, hoping to come up with a bomb I could throw back at him. But what was I to say—*Who says I'm a jerk?* No, only a jerk would say that. On the other hand something inside wouldn't let me agree with him, so I ended up saying, "Oh, nothing, forget it," and I hung up. I can't say I hadn't entertained the idea of talking to Paul before Tony called, bcause I had, so maybe I wasn't a complete jerk, but right now I didn't know how or when to do it.

At dinner that night I pushed my food back and forth across my place, a sure sign that something was wrong. I could tell my mother wanted to ask me what was the matter, but she must have known it was better to leave me alone. When dessert came, I expected my father to ask me if I wanted to talk to him after dinner. For some reason tonight he waited for an hour before he came up to my room.

"Do you want to talk?"

I stopped doing my homework to look up just long enough to say no.

"I'll be around if you want to talk later," he said.

"There's nothing to talk about," I snapped, surprising myself by the force of my answer. I watched him leave my room and go downstairs. What was I supposed to tell him? After all, how do you tell your father you've made a complete mess of your life? How do you tell him about parts of yourself which you are very ashamed of and wish would never express themselves but did? *Dad, ever since Tony moved into the neighborhood I've had the feeling that Paul's been spending more time with him than me, and then the other night at the dance when I saw him with Ellen . . . well, I was so angry at him, I really wanted to hurt him bad. Aren't you proud of me?* It was hard enough admitting it to myself. How could I ever admit it to him—or to anybody else, for that matter? Right now things seemed pretty hopeless.

I finished up my math and then went down to the kitchen to get a snack. The silence of the house was occasionally interrupted by the television in the den. As usual, there was nothing to eat in the refrigerator. If I were a rabbit, I probably would have considered what I saw a feast. Lettuce, tomatoes, carrots, sprouts . . . sprouts are like eating grass. Or if I were a mouse . . . mmmm, three cheeses, two of whose names I couldn't even pronounce. And yogurt . . . yecch, the thought of it made me sick. Or some leftover cold meatloaf from tonight . . . not so bad except for the gravy that sort of hardens and forms a jellylike substance on it . . . looking at it gives me chills . . . and then there were some old cold cuts.

"There's nothing in here to eat," I yelled, knowing already what my mother's answer would be.

"There's cheese, cold cuts"—I mouthed the words along with her—"yogurt, fresh vegetables if you want to make a salad, and there's some leftover meatloaf from tonight. . . ."

I slammed the refrigerator door in disgust. *She never buys anything that I like. If it isn't nutritious or healthy or packed with all the essential vitamins and minerals, it doesn't stand a prayer of getting into this house. Boy, what I wouldn't do for a big thick cheese steak with extra sauce and onions or a deluxe Italian hoagie with extra mayonnaise and peppers.*

". . . And I think there's a frozen pizza in the freezer."

"Pizza," I muttered to myself. At least I wouldn't starve tonight. I found the pizza behind two frozen chickens and put it in the oven. While I was wondering what to do for the next twenty minutes, my father came into the kitchen, supposedly to get a drink of water. Now more than ever I wanted someone to talk to, but I wasn't sure whom I needed to talk to or who I wanted it to be. I was so confused about my feelings at this point that I don't think I would have known the right person if he came up and bit me. "It sure gets quiet here when Robbie and Sally are sleeping," I said, trying to force some conversation.

"Two of the couples we play bridge with are away on business, so the game was canceled."

"Oh," I said. I'd run completely out of things to ask. My father paused a second, looking at first as if he wanted to say something and then as if he wanted me to continue, and when nothing happened, he disappeared into the den.

"Dad," I yelled—probably just as he was sitting down.

"What do you want, Richie?"

"Dad . . . what's on TV now?"

"Some spy movie," he replied. I heard him ask my mother the name. "We both missed the beginning."

"Okay, thanks," I said in an uncharacteristically formal way as I stared up at the kitchen clock. Fifteen minutes to go until pizza time. "Dad." The word slipped out before I had a chance to stop it.

"Yeah?"

Maybe I'd never wanted to stop it. "Can I talk to you

for a second?" I smelled the odor of his pipe getting stronger and then he appeared in the doorway. He pulled up a chair beside me, not too close so that I felt crowded, but close enough to let me feel his presence. "Did you ever hate yourself when you were growing up?"

"Sometimes I even hate myself now," he said with a reassuring smile.

"No. I mean really hate yourself," I repeated, making sure he understood the question.

"For something you did?" he asked.

"Not actually did, but almost." I could see that my father had no idea what I was talking about, and I had to make a quick decision now whether or not to work up the courage to explain it to him. "Did you ever think something horrible about someone else?" I paused again, but my father still looked puzzled, so I continued. "You know, the other night at the dance when Paul and I got into that fight? Well, I really wanted to hurt him bad." I drew my neck down into my collar and hunched up my shoulders as if to protect myself from an expected slap. None was forthcoming. "I don't think you heard what I just said," I told him, starting to feel myself welling up inside. "I've been so jealous of Paul's relationship with Tony that I thought of hurting him bad the other night and almost did!"

My father wrapped his arm around my shoulders and gave me a reassuring squeeze. "You know, there's a big difference between thinking about something and actually doing it." I don't know if that was supposed to make me feel good or not, but if it was, it sure failed miserably. "You act as if you're the only one in the world who ever had thoughts like these." How did he know that? "I hate to burst your bubble, but you don't corner the market on jealousy or bad thoughts, or probably anything, for that matter."

15

I could have probably continued avoiding Paul the rest of the week if it weren't for biology lab. You see, we'd chosen each other as lab partners at the beginning of the year, thinking that it would make lab a real ball. And it had been, up to now. Today it would probably be a horror show. We looked at each other briefly when we entered the lab but said nothing as we took our seats. There in front of us, with its arms and legs pinned down to keep it from sliding around in the wax-lined tray, was a large, slimy frog.

Mrs. Singer, our biology teacher, stood up at the front of the room and waited a second for the *yecchs* and *grosses* to die down before she gave us our instructions. "Today we are going to dissect a frog."

"There's no way I'm going to touch that thing," said the girl in the seat next to mine to her partner.

"Follow the directions for the dissection as outlined in your lab book. I'll be around to help anyone who needs it."

Out of the corner of my eye I saw Paul look at me. "Like it or not, we have to do this lab, so if you're not going to talk to me, I'll read the instructions and you can tap once for yes and twice for no. Okay?" Still looking straight ahead, I tapped once on the desk. "Okay, do you want to turn to page a hundred ten or should I?" Paul waited for my response until he realized he hadn't asked a yes-or-no question. "Oh, yeah, do you want to turn to page a hundred ten?" I tapped two times. "Then I should?" Tap! Paul turned to page 110 and laid the book down between us. "Are you going to dissect or should—no, do you want to dissect today?" Tap! Next to the pan were a pair of forceps and a scissors, which I took as I waited for further instructions. "At point X in figure twenty-three dash one, grip the skin with the forceps. Cut the skin in the order shown by the numbered dotted lines. Pull the skin up while you cut with a scissors. Open the skin up and pin it down, angled away from the animal." Paul paused, waiting for me to begin.

I looked at the picture in the book and then at the frog. Tap! Tap!

"I thought you wanted to dissect," asked Paul. Tap! "Then what is it?" I pointed at the frog's belly and then at the X in the picture. Paul continued to have a puzzled look on his face. "What? You do want to do it?" Tap! "Then do it." I got a piece of paper from my notebook and wrote something on it which I passed to him. Paul opened the paper and read THERE IS SOMETHING WRONG WITH OUR FROG. "What's wrong with it?" asked Paul. I again pointed to the X and then to our frog. Paul shrugged his shoulders. I took the paper back and wrote THERE IS NO X ON OUR FROG'S STOMACH. HOW DO I KNOW WHERE TO CUT? Paul read the note and then got up and walked to the front of the

room. He returned with a black Magic Marker in his hand and promptly drew a large X on the frog. "Is that good enough or do you want me to draw in all the dotted lines too?"

"No, the X is fine," I said with a smile on my face. I wanted to do a good job with this dissection, so I took my time, and while I worked, Paul read to me from the book. "It says here that the term *frog* is commonly applied to those forms with long legs and smooth mucus-covered skins, *toad* being used for a variety of robust, short-legged types, especially with rough skins."

"Need any help, boys?"

"No, thanks, Mrs. Singer." I waited until she'd moved away before pointing in her direction and asking, "Frog or toad?"

"How short do her legs have to be?" asked Paul.

"Next time she comes by, see if her skin is smooth or rough!"

"It says here that people in various parts of the world eat frogs' legs."

"I wonder if there is a special pond for crippled frogs?"

Paul started to laugh out loud, and he had to cover his mouth when the teacher looked back at us. "Listen to this. 'Most frogs are considered to be placid animals, but recent observations have shown that some species exhibit aggressive tendencies, especially at breeding time. Male bullfrogs defend their territories against intrusion by other males by kicking, bumping, and biting. One South American frog has a long, sharp spine on the thumb which he uses to wound other males when wrestling.'"

"Let me see that," I said, grabbing the book out of Paul's hand.

"There," said Paul.

"'Most frogs are considered to be placid animals . . .'"

Hmmm. It was there, all right, just as he'd said. I turned toward Paul and widened my eyes as I looked him square in the face. My jaw dropped open and my tongue darted in and out of my mouth. Then, without warning, I let out a loud, deep *"Rib-it! Rib-it!"*

"Are you okay, Mr. Harmon?"

"Oh, yes, Mrs. Singer," I said with a straight face, feeling my skin tone changing from pink to red to flaming red to embarrassment red. "I must have gotten a frog caught in my throat." Paul lost it completely after that, jumping up and claiming, so that he wouldn't get tossed out of class, that he had to go to the bathroom. When he finally returned, the dissection was finished, and we spent the rest of the period on our best behavior—mainly because Mrs. Singer was standing behind us. When the bell rang, Paul and I walked out of class together on our way to lunch.

"Look over there," I said, pointing with my head. "Frog or toad?"

"Frog!"

I nodded my agreement. Paul pointed to another one.

"Definitely toad!" We frogged and toaded our way to the lunchroom and sat down at our table.

"What about that one over there?" I asked.

"Enough," said Paul. "I'd like to have a serious talk with you."

"Okay," I said, not really being one for serious talks. "Talk to me seriously."

"Come on, Richie," said Paul, somewhat annoyed.

"Okay, no more jokes."

"What's happened to you since the summer?"

I paused for a second, trying to get all my thoughts together in a coherent way so Paul would understand what had happened. It wasn't easy.

"Mind if I join you guys?" It was Tony.

"Richie and I would like to be alone today," said Paul.

"Okay," said Tony. "See you guys later."

"Well?" said Paul, reminding me it was my turn to speak.

I cleared my throat and reluctantly began to talk. "How would you feel if you came home from camp and saw that your best friend didn't like you as much anymore?"

"That's not true," interrupted Paul. He'd jumped up from the table.

"Will you sit down and let me finish?" Paul nodded and sat down. "Every time I called or tried to come over, you were with Tony."

"I was not!"

This time I just stared at Paul and he got quiet. "It seemed like I was second best and I didn't like it." Paul opened his mouth, but I didn't let him say a thing, continuing, "Then there was the time in the locker room when I came down and the two of you were talking and I asked what it was about and you said nothing. You just didn't want me to know. And then there was the time at soccer practice that you put your nose in where it didn't belong and Chuck ended up biting me in the head and then I told you not to tell and you did and then there was the incident of you and Ellen at the dance." I paused to take a deep breath. "Do you blame me for feeling angry and left out?"

"Are you finished now?" asked Paul. I nodded.

"First of all, there's no way I'm going to accept the blame for Chuck biting you. Second, I already apologized for telling. Third, just because I spend some time with another kid doesn't mean I like you less. I don't have to spend twenty-four hours a day with you to show you I still like you as much. Don't you think all the times we spent together before count for anything? Believe it or not, Tony likes you, too, and there may be times that just the two of you will do something without me. Is everything okay now?"

Paul had said too many things too quickly. They all sounded okay. They made sense. I needed a little time to digest everything. "Yeah, sure," I said hesitantly. If I hadn't paused, I might have been able to pull it off.

"You don't sound convinced," said Paul.

"No, I am, really."

Paul looked at me for a second and, knowing that this was not the time to press things further, got up from the table. "I'll call you tonight," he said.

"Call around eight."

"I think we're going out for dinner, so I'll probably call around eight-thirty."

"Fine!"

"Or maybe I'll call at six-thirty before we go."

"Fine!"

"Or five-thirty if we—"

"Get out of here," I yelled. Laughing, I picked up a cracker and tossed it at his head. It missed by a mile. Maybe things would be okay now. Maybe they would.

16

Whoever invented the basketball was a very wise person. It has so many uses besides just the game itself. I find that when I'm angry I can throw it against a wall or a door or just up in the air, and after a few times I'm not angry anymore. Sometimes just making a difficult shot or making a lot of shots in a row makes me feel good about myself. Or like today, just shooting around makes me forget school or even this thing with Paul. And just to make sure I wasn't bothered by anybody, I went to the court that no one uses, behind the elementary school. Nothing was going in for me, but that didn't seem to matter. I pictured myself in the championship game grabbing the rebound with three seconds to go and powering up the ball to put in the winning basket.

"Nice shot." I looked up. It was Chuck. Couldn't he leave me alone? All I wanted today was to be alone. "I've been practicing what you showed me the other day. Give me the ball and I'll show you." I don't know why, but I flipped him the ball and he caught it and drove in for a perfect lay-up. "Well, what do you think?"

"Great," I said, hoping that this would satisfy him.

Chuck retrieved the ball and then started to walk out toward the left of the foul line. From where I was standing it looked to me as if he were actually counting the number of steps he took. "This is my spot," he said, proudly pointing to an imaginary spot on the court. "I can't miss from here."

I had never seen Chuck so cocky before, but I figured after one or two misses he would go back to his wimpy old self and leave. So I said, "Bet you can't make five in a row."

"Okay," he said, still brimming with confidence. "What are we betting for?"

"Anything you want," I said smugly.

"If I win, you have to teach me how to shoot a jump shot."

"And if you lose, you'll leave me alone, okay?"

"Sure," said Chuck as he let his first shot fly. Swish. *Beginner's luck,* I thought. I retrieved the ball and tossed it back to him. Swish. Before I'd had time to turn around, the second one was in the basket. *He'll never make three,* I thought. Swish. Swish. "One more," he reminded me, and then threw up the fifth shot. As the ball went through the hoop I felt like a city slicker who had just been sucked in by a con man.

"Jump-shot time," he said with a smile on his face.

"Where did you learn to do that?"

"I was here the other day just practicing what you showed me and I just threw up the ball from here and . . ." Swish. Six in a row. Chuck was unbelievable. "I put in fifteen in a row yesterday."

"Show me how you do that."

"It's easy. You just stand right here and . . ." Swish. Seven in a row. I got the ball again and Chuck pointed to an imaginary spot on the ground. "First, come over here and put both feet right here and just throw the ball up like this and . . ."

I grabbed the ball right out of his hands just as he was about to shoot. Eight in a row would have been too much to bear. I studied the basket and was just about to shoot when Chuck tapped me on the shoulder and said, "Just throw it up, like this." Swish. Eight. The next time I made sure Chuck stood back so I could take the shot. I guess I pushed the ball a little too hard the first time, because it hit the heel of the rim and bounced back. "Too hard," said Chuck. "A little bit lighter next time and I think you'll have it."

"I thought I was supposed to be the teacher today," I said, surprised at the turnabout.

"You will be in just a second. Now, softer this time." I let the ball roll off my fingers and this time it went right in.

"Not bad for the first time," said Chuck with a smile.

"You know, you've really changed over the past two years."

"I was going to say the same thing about you too," said Chuck.

"I used to think you were a real turkey."

"I was," agreed Chuck, to my surprise. "My pop's a nice guy, but he's not too much into sports. I don't have any older brothers, so I had no one to show me the kind of things other kids learn." I think Chuck was sorry he'd said that, because he got real quiet afterward. I know I was sorry he'd said it, because I felt like a real jerk for all the teasing and things I had done to him.

"I thought you were going to show me how to shoot a jump shot."

"Huh? Oh, yes. Now stand right here and hold the ball just like . . ."

17

That night I tried to explain to my parents what had happened between Paul and me at lunch and between Chuck and me after school. At first I thought they understood, but when they started talking to me about growing up and changing friendships and other heavy stuff, my mind wandered off and I realized it was up to me to sort things out for myself.

I sort things out best when I have a basketball in my hands, so when fifth period came around the next day, I decided to go to the gym instead of eating lunch. The same question that had kept me up the night before danced around unanswered in my head. What would things be like with Paul now? Was what had happened with Chuck yesterday a fluke?

I threw up a foul shot that only hit net. *Things seem terribly complicated in the beginning. But they always manage to work themselves out, so why worry?* I retrieved the ball and shot a short jumper from the corner. It missed. *What if this is the time they don't?* I kicked the ball in anger and it landed in the top row of section W and then proceeded to bounce down row by row to center court before it stopped.

The sound of hands clapping behind me was the first clue I had that anyone else was in the gym. The voice was unmistakably Chuck's. "That would have been right through the uprights if you had been kicking a field goal."

"Oh, hi," I said. I retrieved the ball and returned to the foul line. "Did you come here to practice your jumper?"

"No," he answered in a very serious tone. "I looked for you first in the lunchroom, and when I didn't see you, I thought you might be here. I wanted to thank you again for yesterday. I really had a great time."

I felt sort of embarrassed by his comments. All I'd done was show him how to shoot a jump shot. There's really nothing special about that.

"It's hard to convince people you've changed when they won't spend any time around you to see that you have. Listen, I have to go." As Chuck turned to leave I thought about how bad I had felt when I thought Paul didn't like me as much as he had before, and then I realized how bad Chuck must feel all the time. I guess it takes a kid to understand how another kid feels. Parents may have the right words, but kids have the feelings.

"Want to shoot around some?" I asked, flipping Chuck the ball. Chuck caught it and walked over to his spot. He let the ball fly and it hit nothing but net again.

"I can do it from the other side too. Here, look, I'll show you." Swish.

"Would you like to learn how to shoot a foul shot?"

"Would I!" said Chuck as he retrieved the ball.

"Here. Stand next to me and hold the ball like this," I

said, positioning his hands on either side of the ball as I spoke.

"You're teaching that wimp how to play basketball?"

I instinctively grabbed the ball out of Chuck's hands as if that would erase the previous scene and turned to face Paul and Tony. "How did you know I was here?" I asked. Out of the corner of my eye I saw Chuck slowly start to take small steps backward.

"You told Paul and me on the bus that you wouldn't be at lunch today and instead you probably would be here shooting baskets in the gym."

Boy am I dumb, I thought, as I pictured the exact scene Tony had just described. *If I wanted to be alone, why did I broadcast to them where I would be? Bigmouth strikes again.* By now Chuck was a good four feet away from me, leaving me alone to face Paul and Tony.

"Paul and I started to eat lunch, but we both decided we'd rather shoot around than eat, so we came here looking for you."

I flipped the ball to Paul, hoping he would take a shot and forget about the question he had asked. "Your shot," I said, forcing a smile. Paul obliged by putting up a jump shot from the key. Tony grabbed the rebound. I glanced over in Chuck's direction and saw he was almost halfway out of the gym. I felt bad, but didn't think this was the time or the place to tell Paul and Tony about Chuck.

"Wanna play a quick game?" asked Tony.

"We need a fourth," chimed in Paul.

"What about him?" I asked, pointing to Chuck, who was just about out the door.

"Are you crazy?" asked Paul.

"He's going to be on my team, so why should it matter to you?" I replied.

Chuck stood completely still, not knowing whether to

leave or return. "It won't even be a contest," said Paul. "But if it's okay with you, it's okay with me. You can take the ball out first."

I knew that the sides weren't fair and that we would probably get run off the court, but as Chuck walked back toward me I told myself *It's only a friendly game, and besides, how badly can they beat us with only fifteen minutes to play?* "Listen, Chuck," I whispered softly in his ear. "I'll throw the ball in to you, you toss it back to me immediately, and then go in toward the basket for the rebound. Remember, I just showed you how to do those shots, and if we are going to have any chance of winning, I have to be the one to shoot."

"Got it, Richie," said Chuck. I could tell it didn't make any difference to him. He was just glad to play.

Paul and Tony placed themselves under the basket. I threw the ball in to Chuck, and he quickly returned the pass to me. As I started to dribble toward the basket, Tony came out to guard me, but Paul stayed where he was, paying no attention to Chuck at all. I faked with my shoulder to the left and drove in past Tony for an easy lay-up. Two to zip. Paul took in the ball first, and received a return pass from Tony. He had a smirk on his face as he literally ran past Chuck and put in an easy lay-up. "Two–two," he said with a smile.

Chuck looked a little unnerved by the way Paul had run past him, and he looked to me for some help. "Just make sure you stand between him and the basket, like this. And make him work a little for his basket."

"Quit stalling," kidded Tony. "We only have about ten minutes more."

We did our standard me-to-Chuck-to-me, only this time I missed the shot and they made theirs, so it was 4–2, their lead. The next time I let Chuck take out the ball, and we passed it around a little more before I shot and tied the score. During the next few turns we traded baskets, and with only three minutes to go we were, surprisingly, still only two points behind.

Then Paul missed an easy short jump shot and Chuck barreled in under the basket and grabbed his first rebound right out of Tony's outstretched hands. He instinctively flipped the ball out to me and I passed it back to him. I cut in toward the basket, hoping to receive a return pass, but instead Chuck tried a lay-up. The shot was like a good-news–bad-news joke. The bad news was that he was too far under the basket and the ball hit the underside of the rim and the rebound hit him in the head. The good news was that from there it bounced directly over to me and I laid it in. "Eight–eight," I said smugly to Paul and Tony.

As Tony took the ball back to half court, I noticed that some other ninth graders had come into the gym; but it didn't seem as if they were paying much attention to us at first. Then I heard some snide comments about Chuck and knew that if I'd heard them, he must have heard them too. Instead of passing the ball, Tony tried a long jump shot that hit the front of the rim and fell into Chuck's hands. Awkwardly but methodically he dribbled back to half court and then back toward the basket. I faked left and moved right without the ball and Chuck hit me with a perfect bounce pass that led to an easy lay-up. "Did you see that pass?" I heard someone say, followed by "Lucky" from another.

"Will you wake up and start guarding him?" snapped Tony.

"You should have stopped that drive!" said Paul in retort.

"You bring the ball in," I said as I flipped Tony the

ball. "Now who's wasting time?" More people had come into the gym, some just to look and others who had gym next period. I think I saw Ellen and Jill and maybe Gina, but I wasn't sure. Tony and Paul seemed to be taking the game a little more seriously, and they had a strategy huddle before taking in the ball this time. The crowd, and it really was a crowd by now, was cheering, a few for Tony and Paul but mostly for Chuck and me.

"Play Paul tight on defense," I yelled. Chuck gave me the thumbs-up sign and stood almost on top of Paul as Tony tried to get the ball in bounds. Chuck came within a hair's breadth of stealing the ball, but Paul managed to secure it close to his chest before passing it behind his back to a cutting Tony. Tony dribbled to the left of the basket and faked once, then twice, before leaping high into the air with a jump shot. As he went up I jumped, too, higher than I ever had before, and I managed to get a piece of the ball, causing it to fall just short of the mark. Chuck gobbled up another rebound and headed back to half court.

"Nice-block," said Tony. The crowd roared their appreciation.

"Thanks," I replied. I posted myself up in the middle, waiting for Chuck to pass me the ball. He bounced the ball in to me perfectly. Out of the corner of my eye I could see Tony overplaying me to the left, and I was sure that with a little fake in that direction I could then go right and have a lay-up that would win the game. I thought I could hear Ellen's voice above everyone else's, yelling, "Score, Richie, score."

I made my fake to the left and Tony took the bait. Why I didn't go right I still don't know. Maybe I was repaying a favor from two summers ago. Maybe I was repaying a favor from today. All I know is, I saw Chuck standing on his spot and I flipped him the ball. Chuck started to pass the ball back, but I stopped him by yelling, "Take *your* shot. Take *your* shot." Chuck seemed surprised at my request and looked very nervous. He fumbled the ball a little as he looked toward the basket. Paul walked out halfway to where Chuck was and waved his arms, egging Chuck on to put up the shot. Chuck took a deep breath before letting the ball fly into the air. A hush came over the crowd as they watched the ball climb to its highest point and then slowly descend as if in slow motion toward the basket and in. Everybody in the gym went absolutely crazy. I was jumping up and down with my fists waving in the air, and so was Chuck, until he was hoisted up onto the shoulders of Tony and Paul, who seemed equally excited about his accomplishment. No one seemed to care about who had won or who had lost. Everyone just felt good.

In the midst of all the excitement and jumping around, I felt someone tap me on the shoulder. I turned to see Ellen. "Richie, you were wonderful," she said, and she threw her arms around me and gave me a big juicy kiss. I could feel my face getting hotter and hotter and my ears felt like they were on fire. At first I thought of pushing her away, but I sort of liked it too.

"Hey, Richie . . . oh, excuse me," said Paul, noticing Ellen for the first time. "I hate to break things up, but we've got to get to class."

"I got to go now," I said to Ellen. "I'll call you tonight."

"Come on, Richie," said Paul. "We'll be late, and you know how Mrs. Singer acts when we get to her class late."

"I'm coming, I'm coming," I said. I looked back at Ellen. "Where's Tony and Chuck?"

"They were here talking about the game just a minute ago," Paul told me. "You know something, Richie? Chuck's shot was lucky."

I guess Paul wanted me to say it wasn't and then he would tell me five reasons he thought it was, but this time I didn't say a word—not because I didn't want to argue with him: I did. But I could argue with him whenever I wanted. The real reason I didn't want to talk was because I was afraid if I did, the feeling from the kiss would disappear, and I wanted to feel that forever.